Why's your name first, Hammy?
HAMMY AND GERBEE
Ask the author, Gerbee!

HAMMY AND GERBEE

MUMMIES AT THE MUSEUM

WONG HERBERT YEE

Christy Ottaviano Books
Henry Holt and Company · New York

Henry Holt and Company,
Publishers since 1866
Henry Holt® is a registered trademark of
Macmillan Publishing Group, LLC
175 Fifth Avenue, New York, NY 10010
mackids.com

Library of Congress Control Number: 2017932702
ISBN 978-1-62779-462-6

Our books may be purchased in bulk for promotional,
educational, or business use. Please contact your local bookseller
or the Macmillan Corporate and Premium Sales Department
at (800) 221-7945 ext. 5442 or by e-mail at
MacmillanSpecialMarkets@macmillan.com.

First edition, 2018/ Designed by April Ward and Sophie Erb

Printed in the United States of America by
LSC Communications, Crawfordsville, Indiana
1 3 5 7 9 10 8 6 4 2

To Judy and Ellen

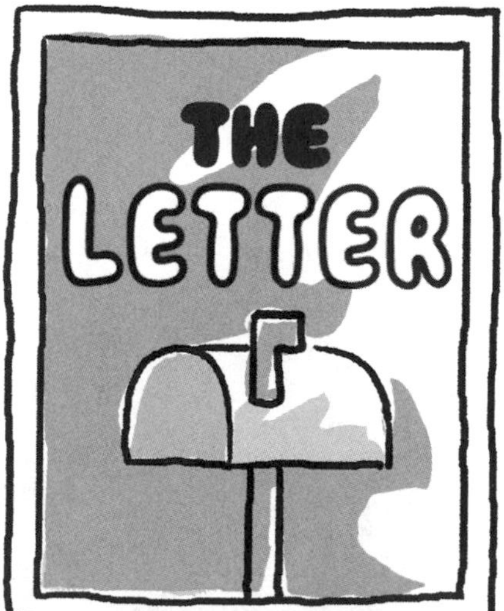
THE
LETTER

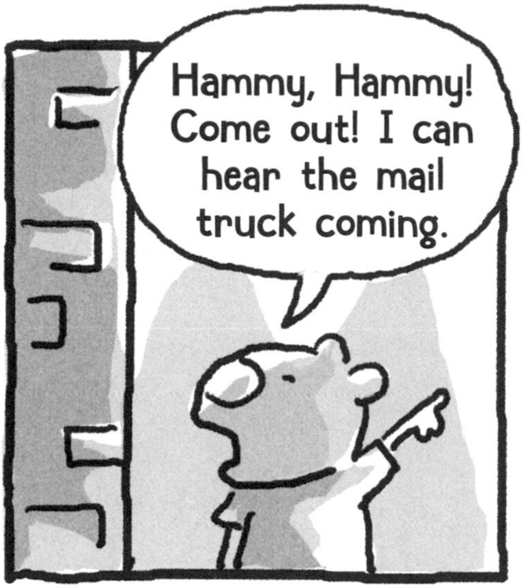
Hammy, Hammy! Come out! I can hear the mail truck coming.

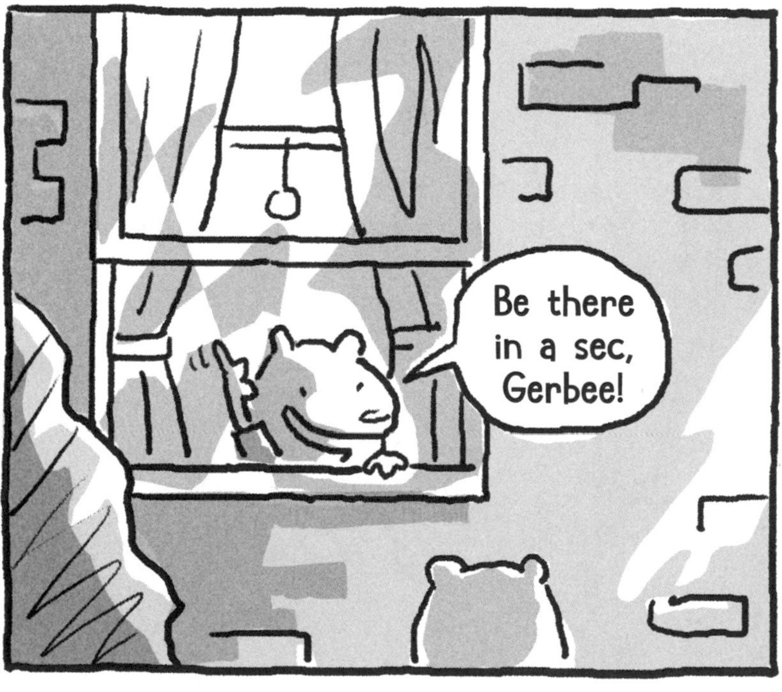
Be there in a sec, Gerbee!

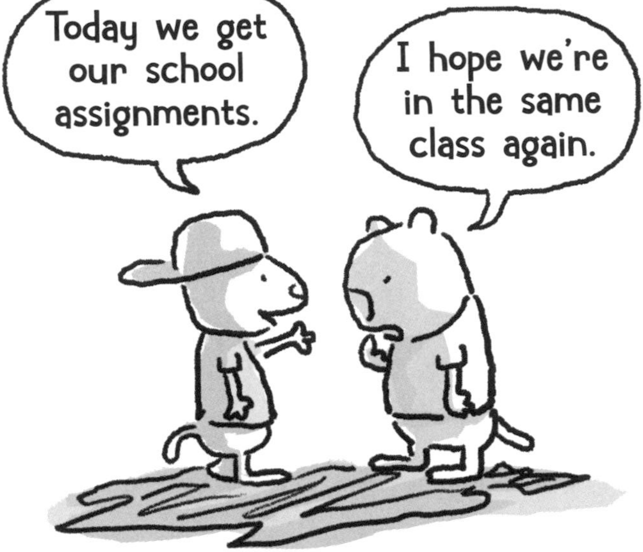
Today we get our school assignments.
I hope we're in the same class again.

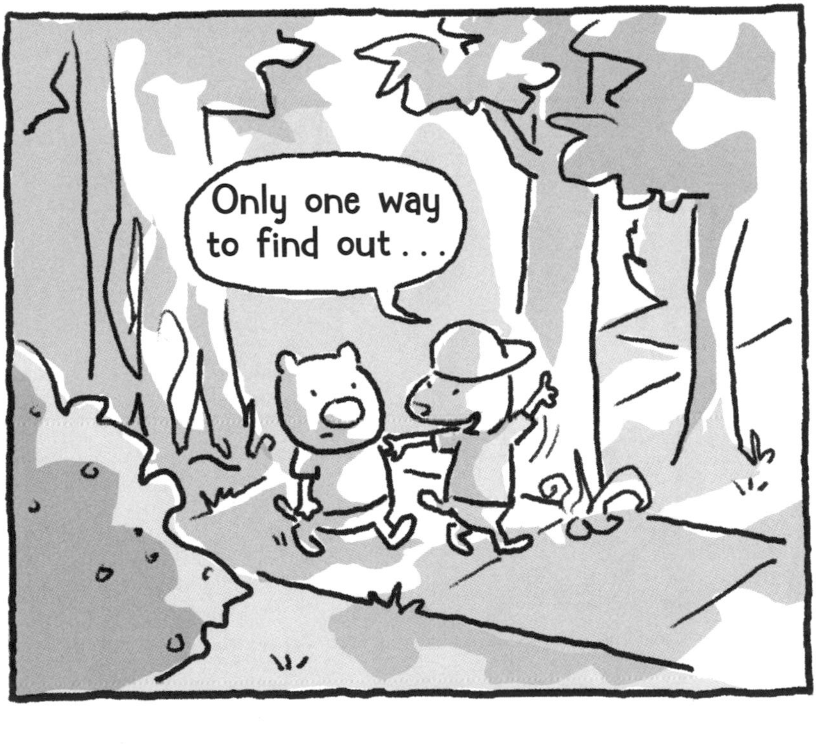
Only one way to find out . . .

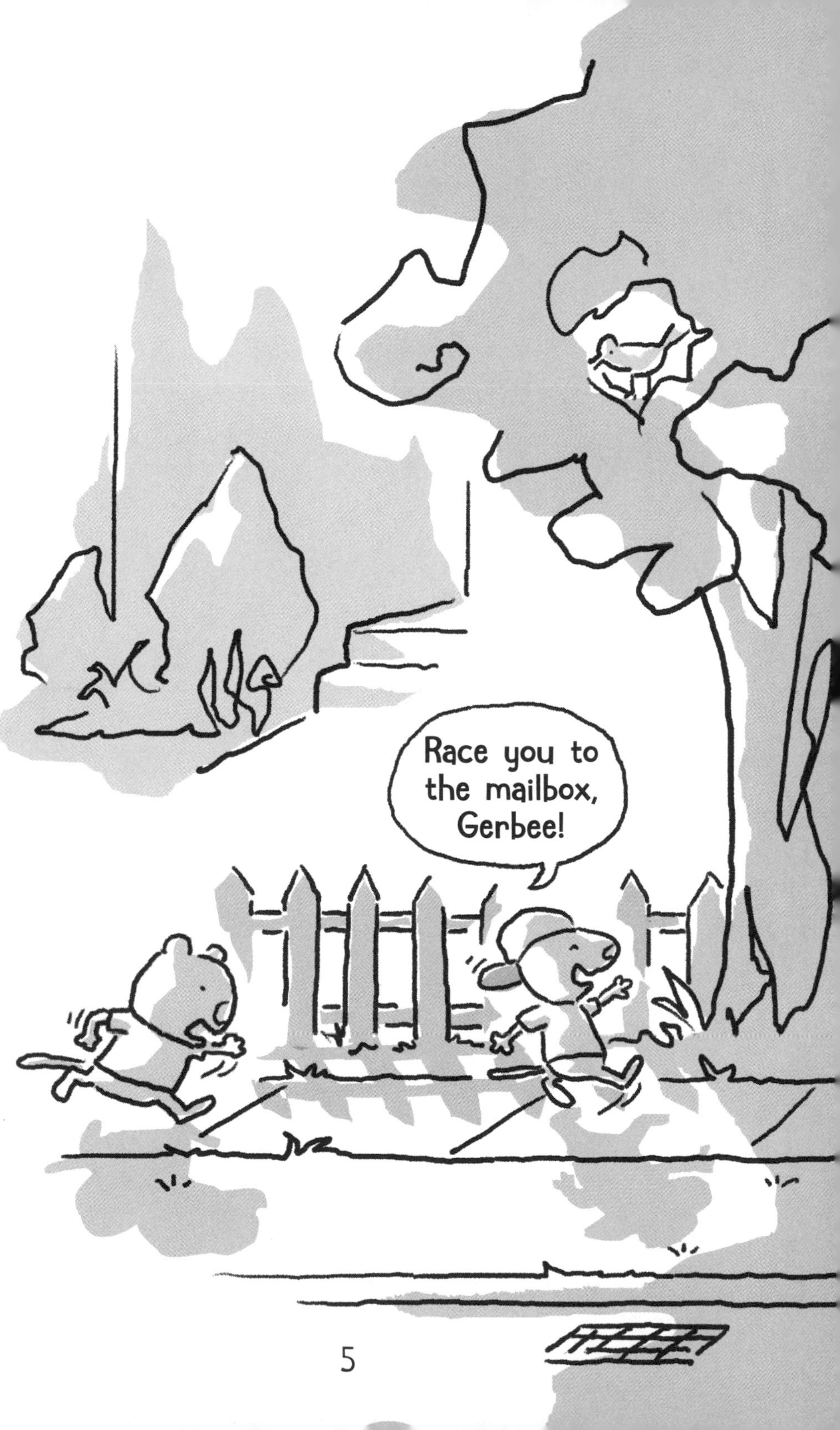
Race you to the mailbox, Gerbee!

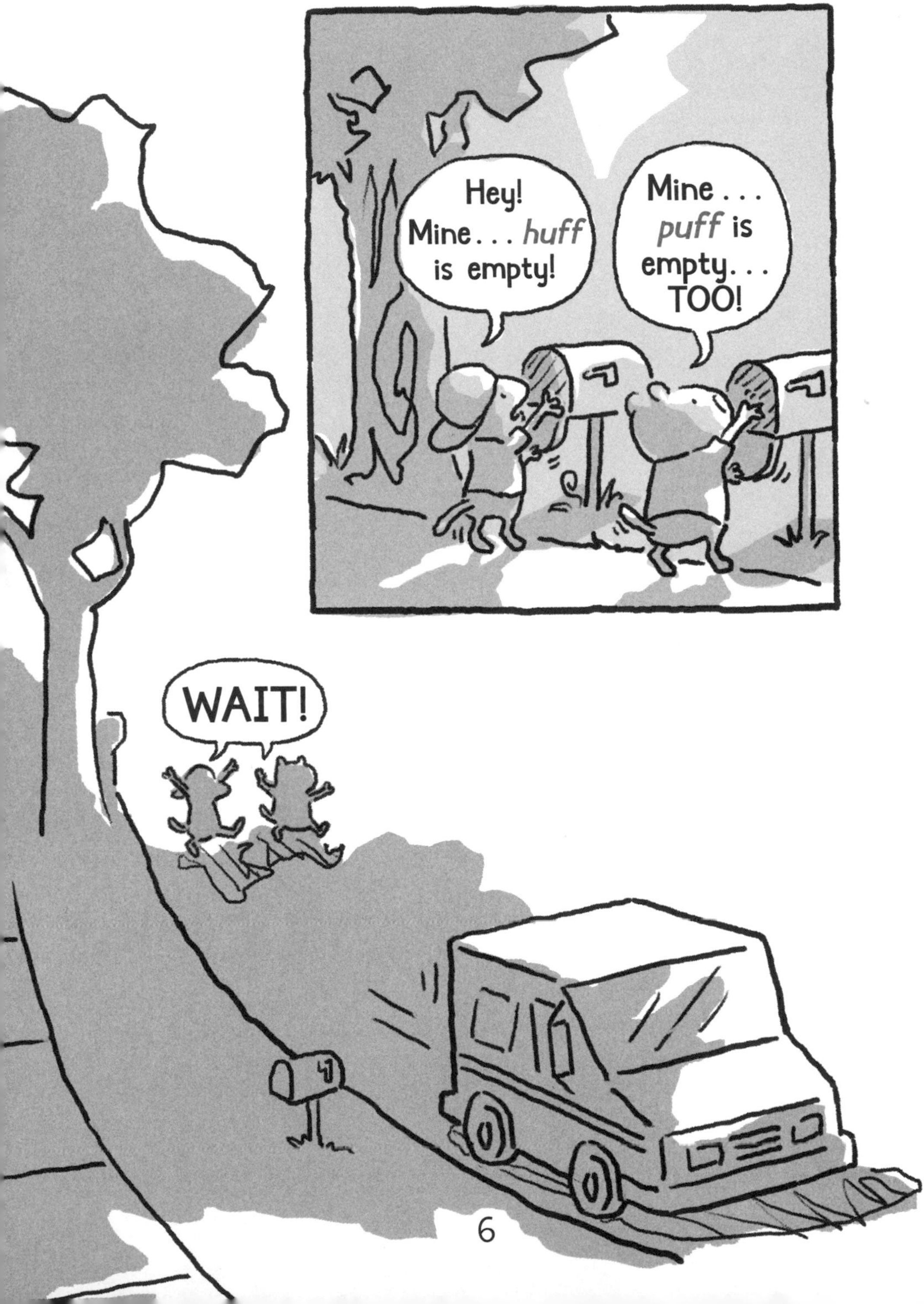
Hey!
Mine . . . huff is empty!
Mine . . . puff is empty. . . TOO!
WAIT!

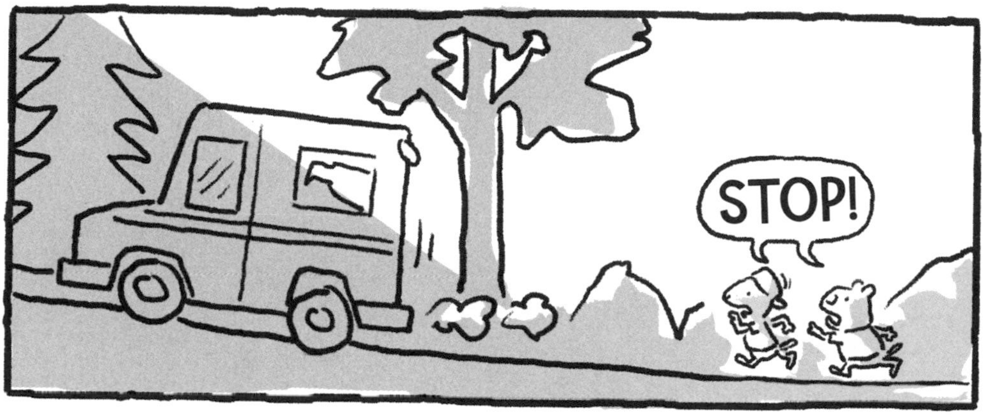
STOP!

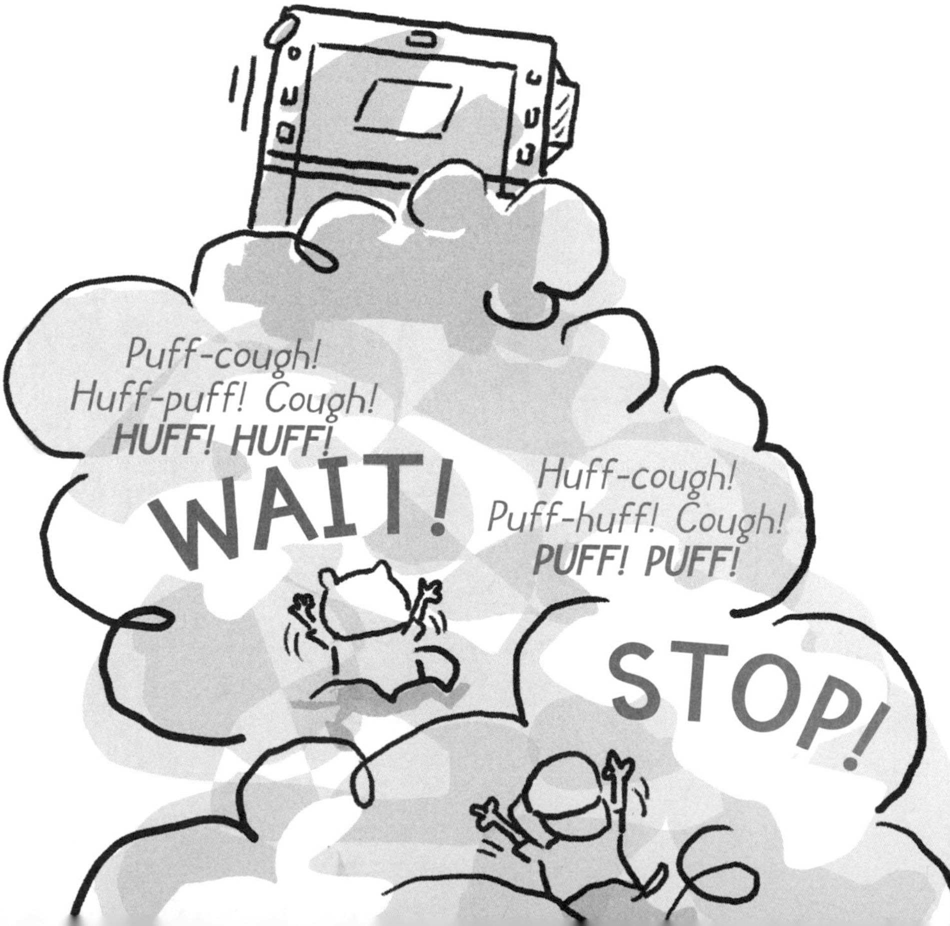
Puff-cough!
Huff-puff! Cough!
HUFF! HUFF!
WAIT!
Huff-cough!
Puff-huff! Cough!
PUFF! PUFF!
STOP!

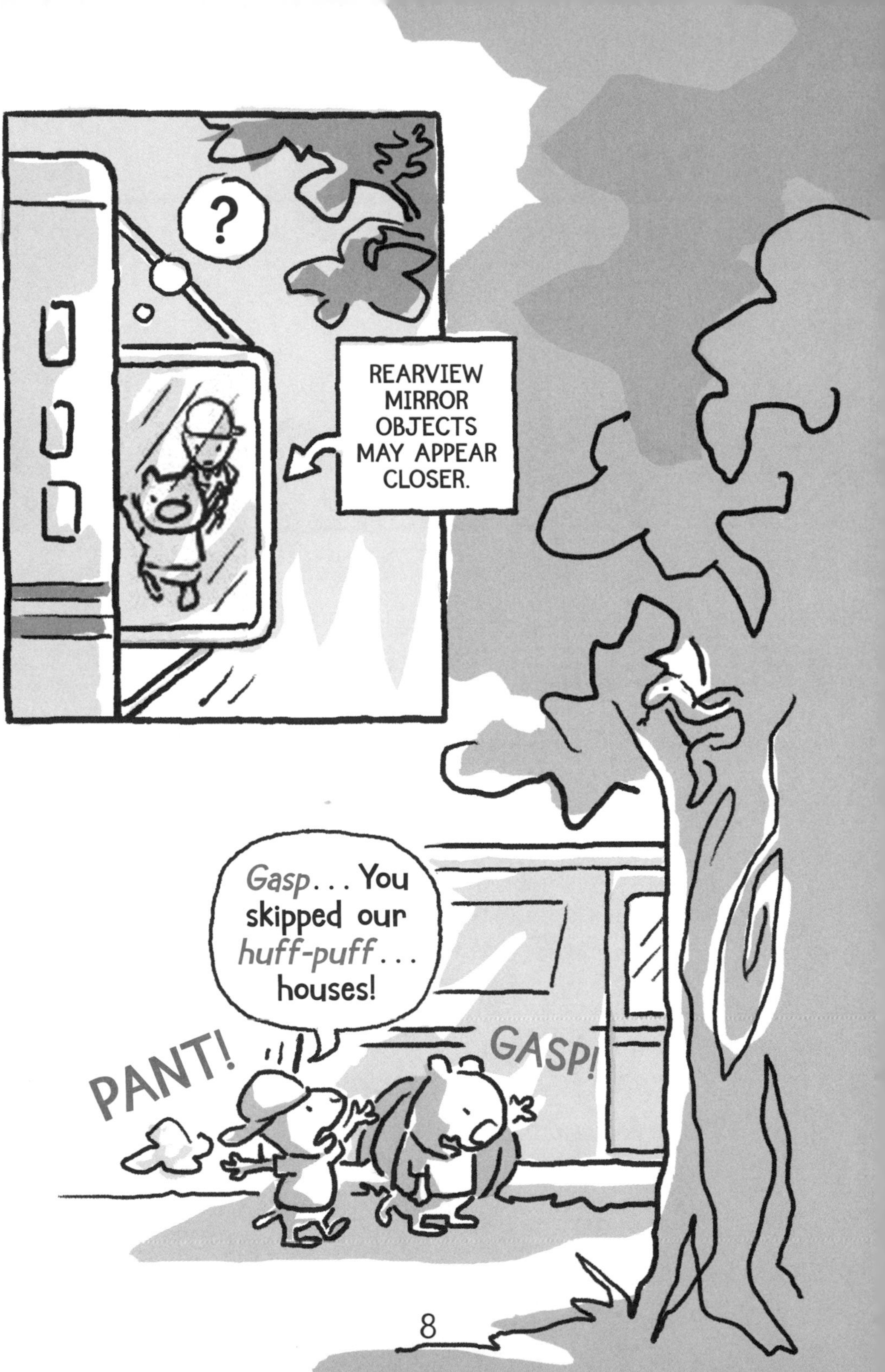
?
REARVIEW MIRROR OBJECTS MAY APPEAR CLOSER.
Gasp... You skipped our *huff-puff*... houses!
PANT!
GASP!

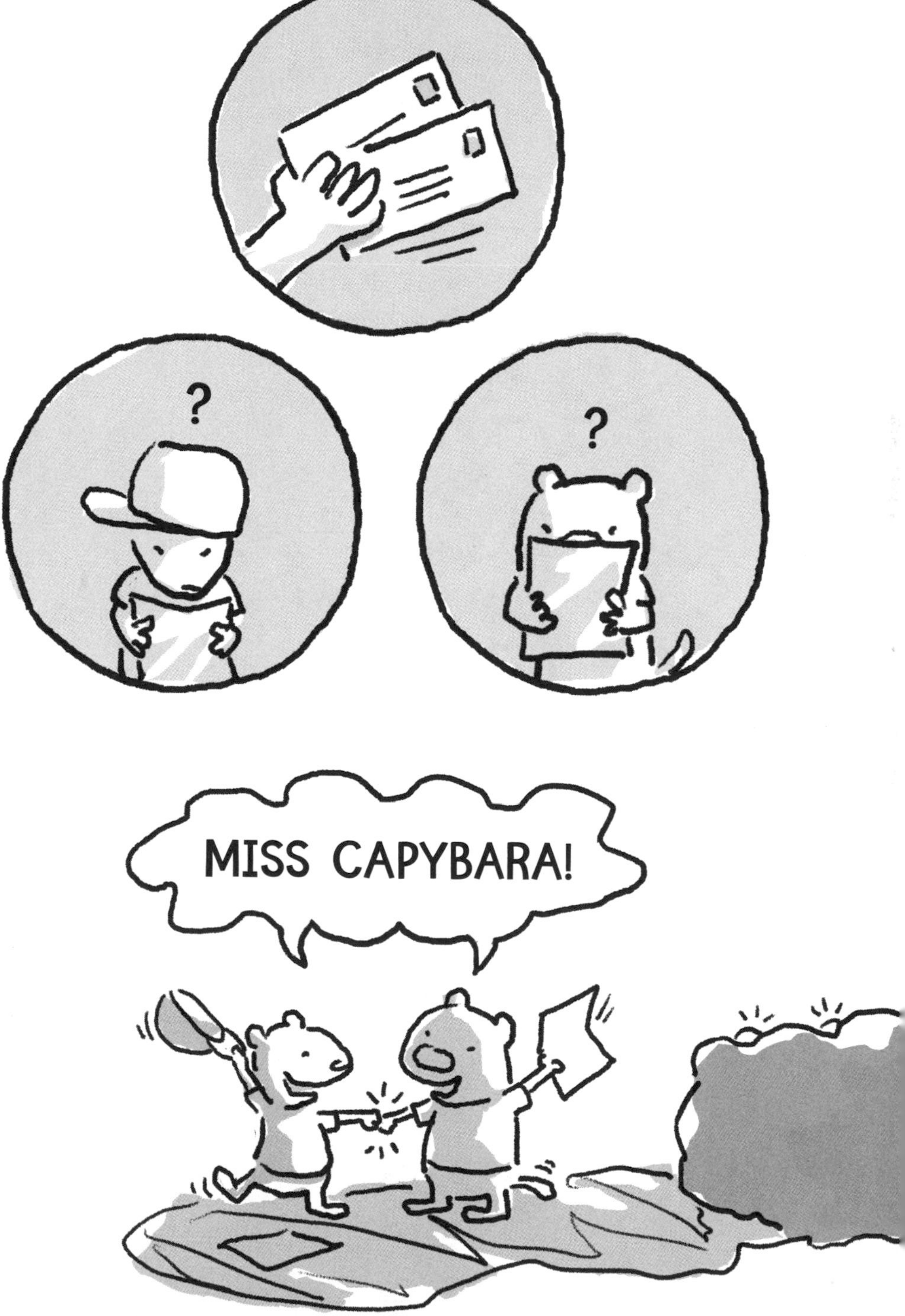
?
?
MISS CAPYBARA!

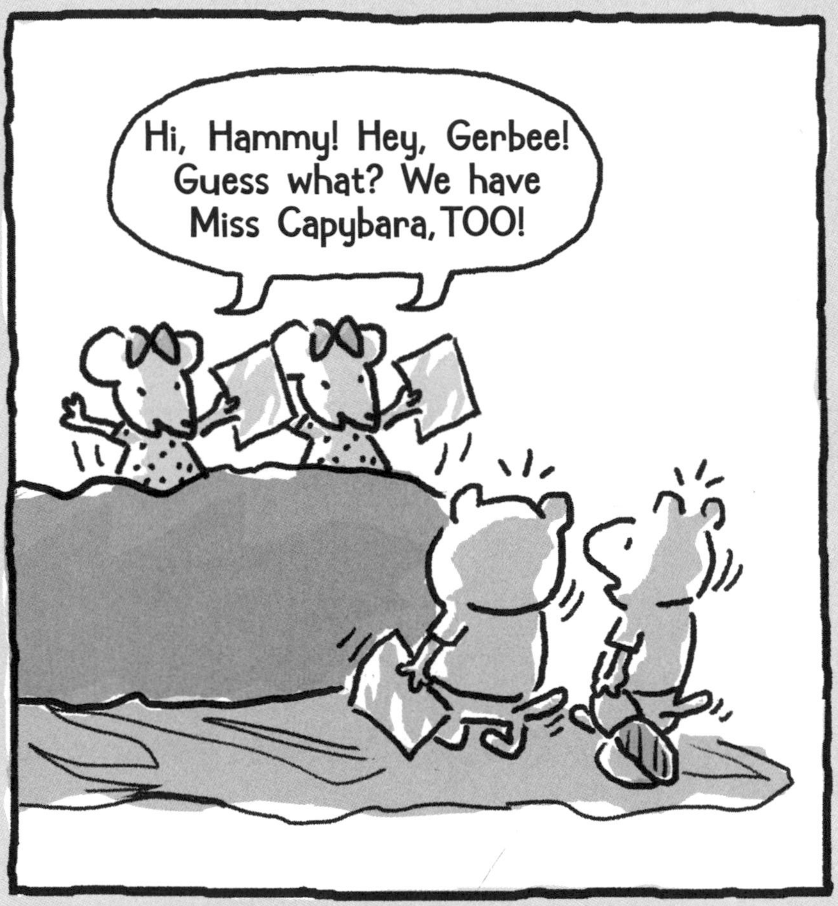
Hi, Hammy! Hey, Gerbee! Guess what? We have Miss Capybara, TOO!

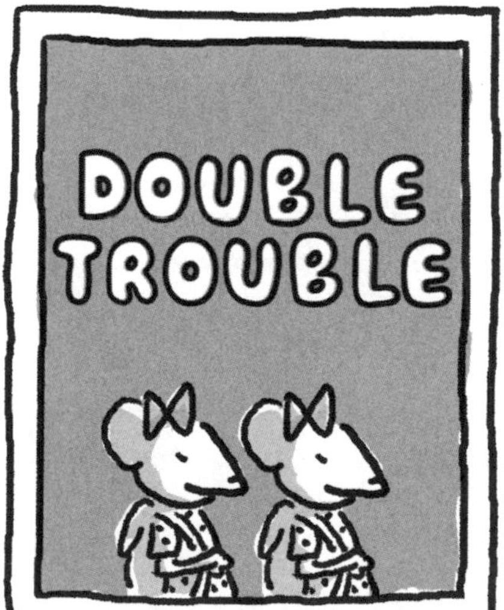
DOUBLE
TROUBLE

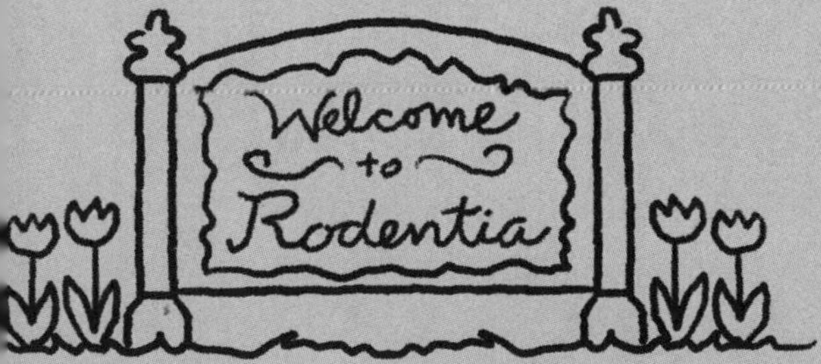
Welcome
to
Rodentia

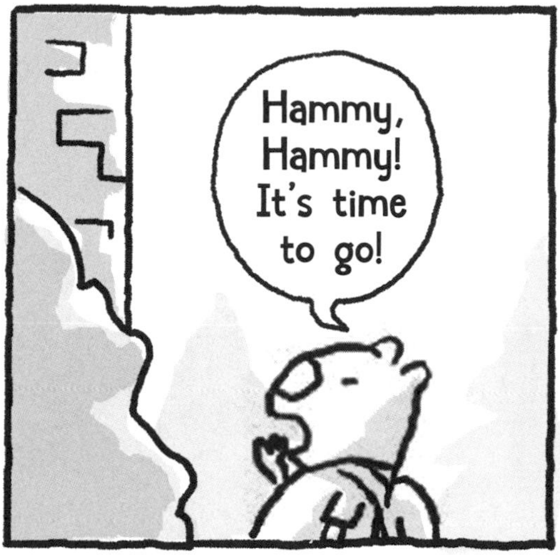
Hammy, Hammy! It's time to go!

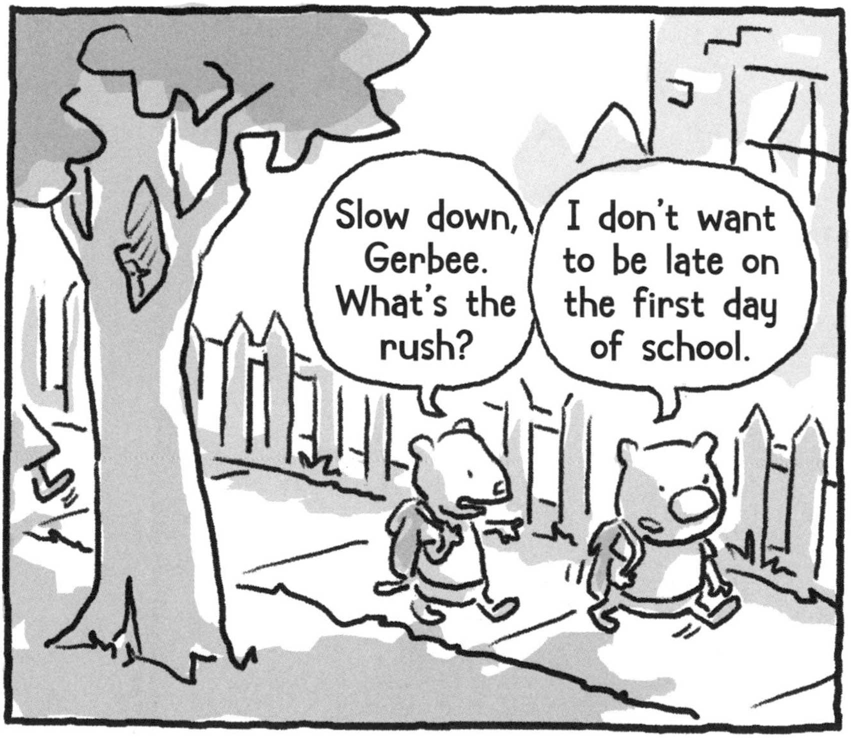
Slow down, Gerbee. What's the rush?
I don't want to be late on the first day of school.

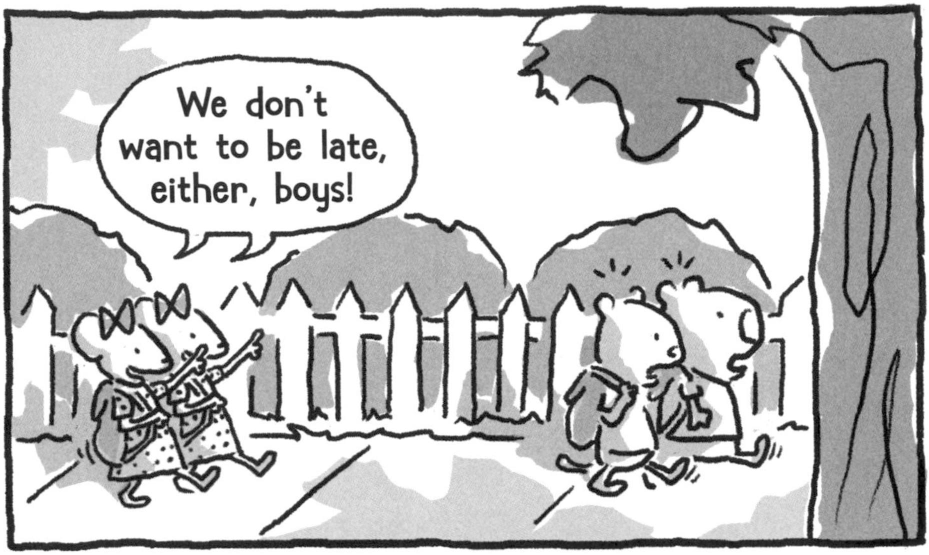
We don't want to be late, either, boys!

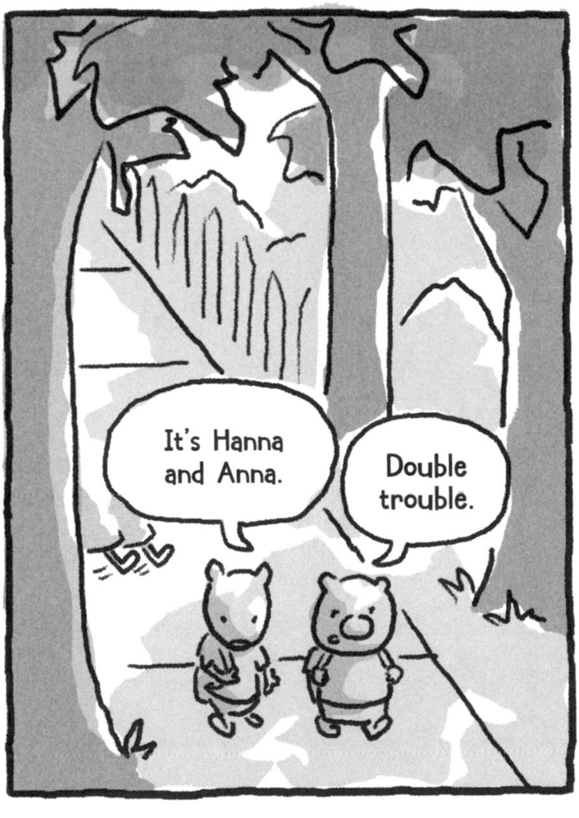
It's Hanna and Anna.
Double trouble.

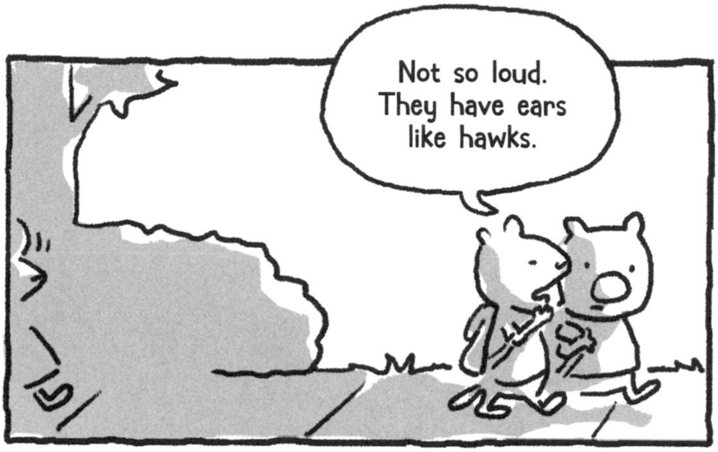
Not so loud. They have ears like hawks.

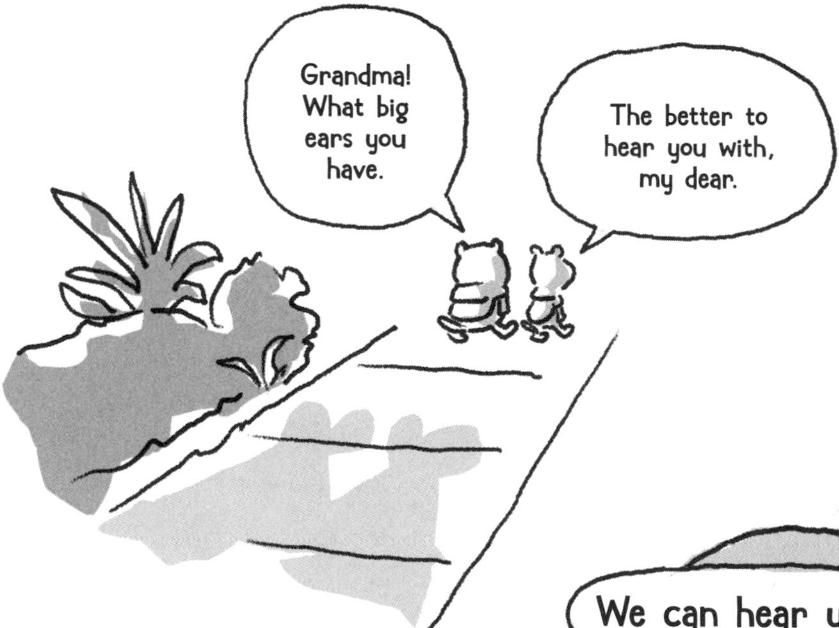
Grandma! What big ears you have.
The better to hear you with, my dear.

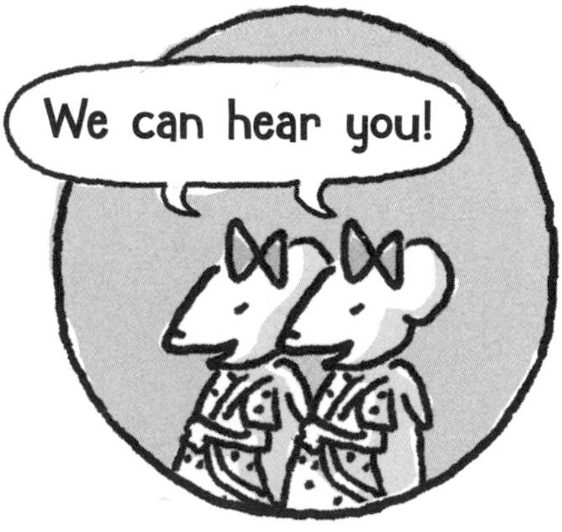
We can hear you!

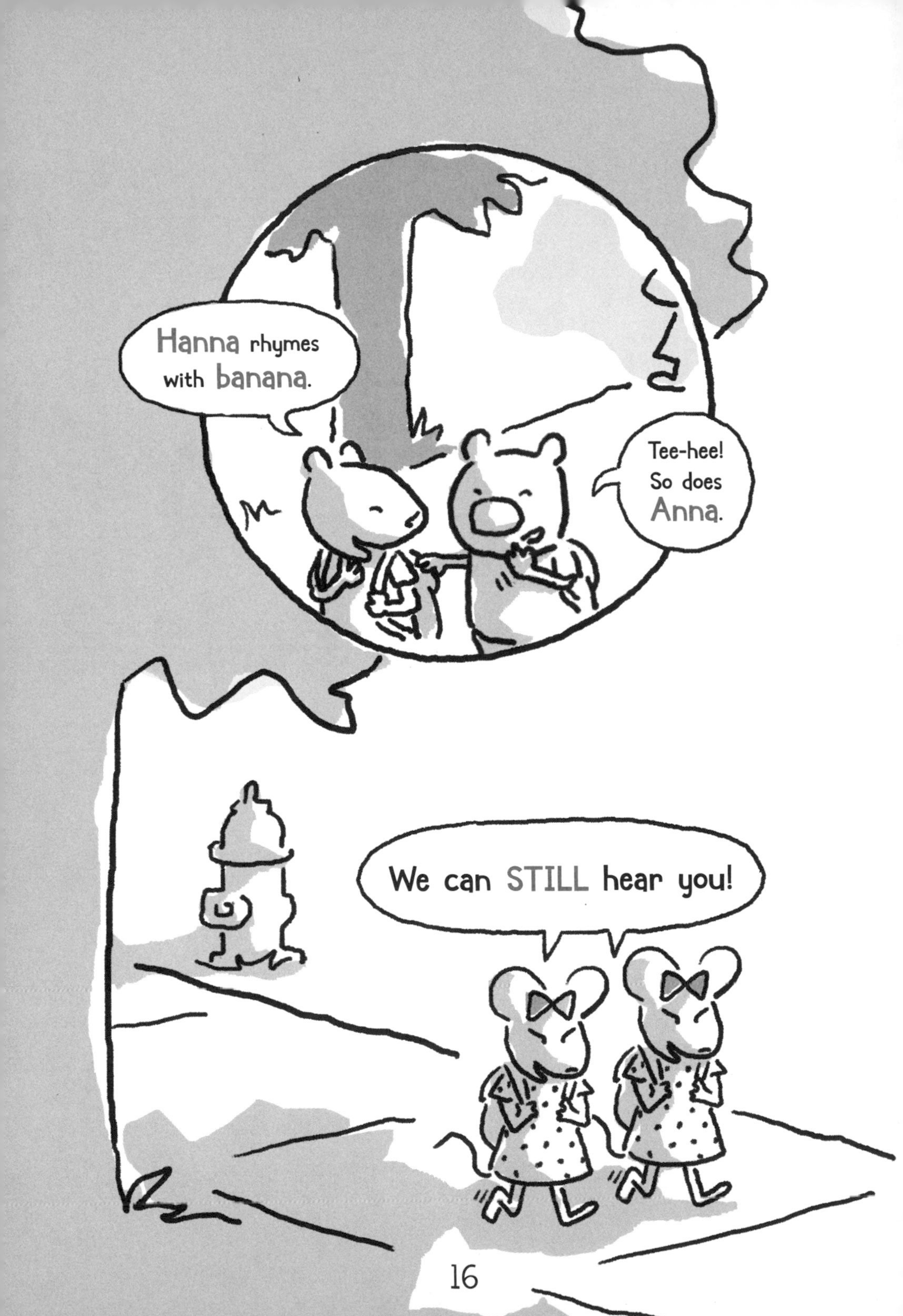
Hanna rhymes with banana.
Tee-hee! So does Anna.
We can STILL hear you!

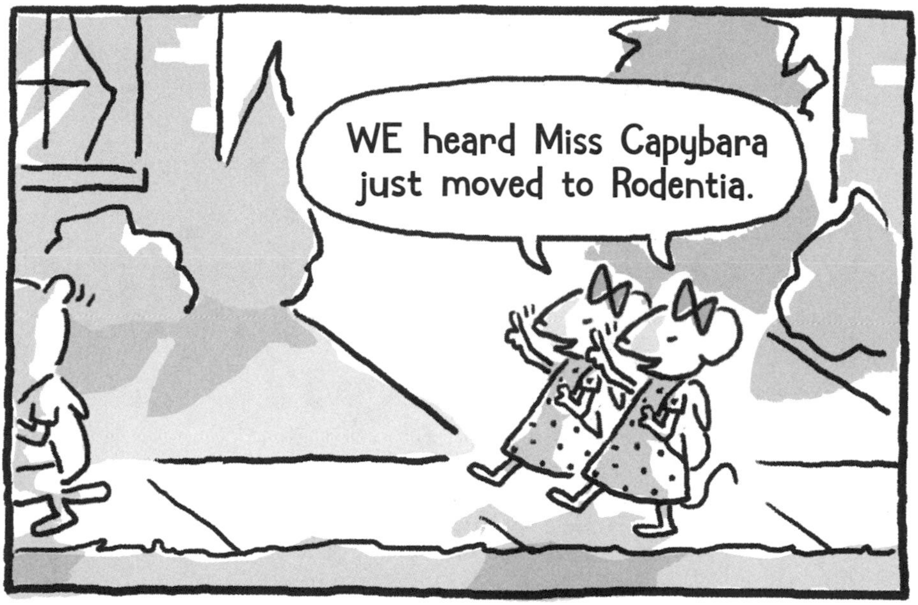
WE heard Miss Capybara just moved to Rodentia.

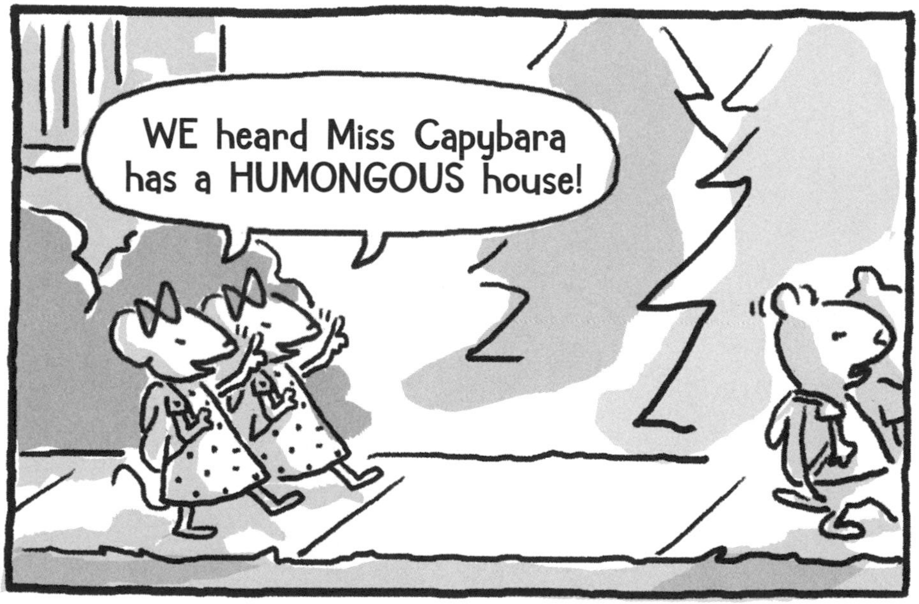
WE heard Miss Capybara has a HUMONGOUS house!

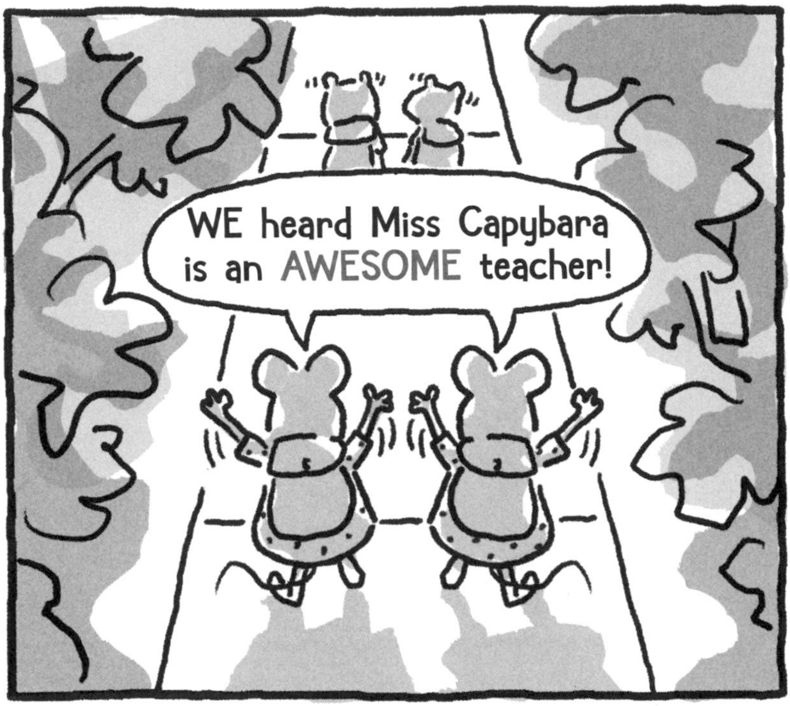
WE heard Miss Capybara is an AWESOME teacher!

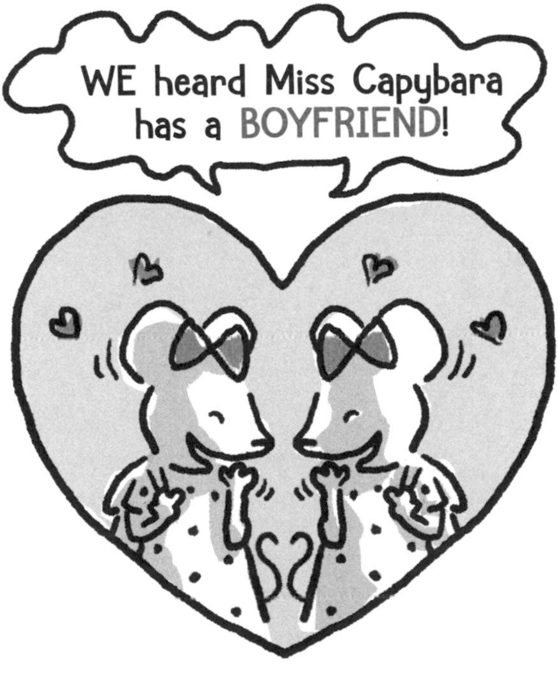
WE heard Miss Capybara has a BOYFRIEND!

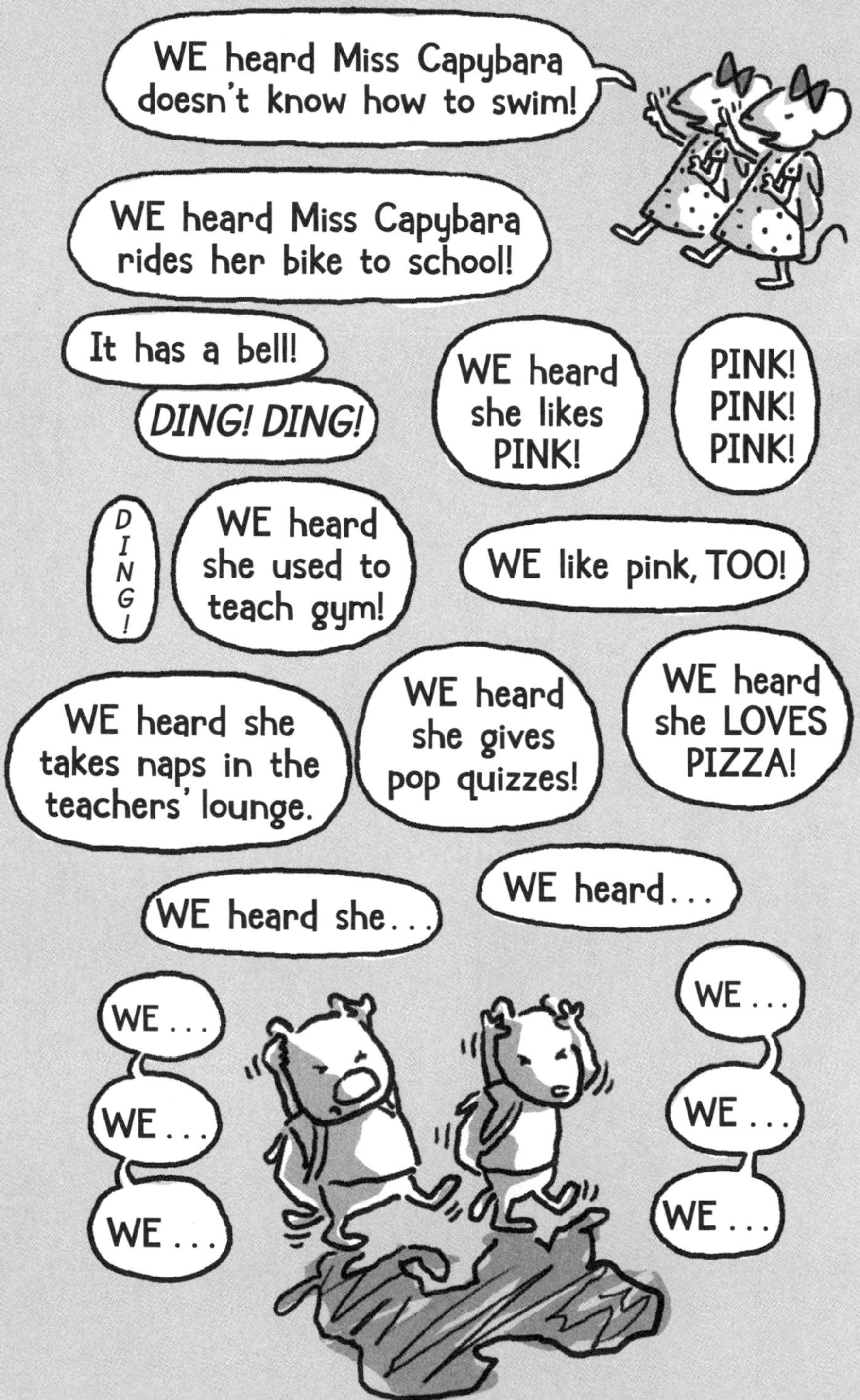

WE heard Miss Capybara doesn't know how to swim!
WE heard Miss Capybara rides her bike to school!
It has a bell!
DING! DING!
WE heard she likes PINK!
PINK! PINK! PINK!
DING!
WE heard she used to teach gym!
WE like pink, TOO!
WE heard she takes naps in the teachers' lounge.
WE heard she gives pop quizzes!
WE heard she LOVES PIZZA!
WE heard she...
WE heard...
WE...
WE...
WE...
WE...
WE...
WE...

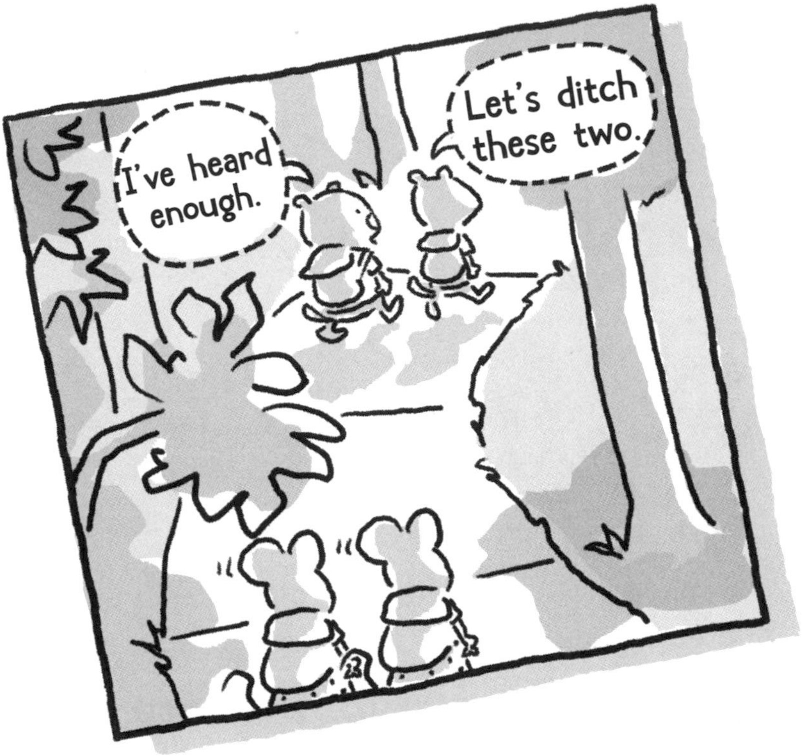
I've heard enough.
Let's ditch these two.

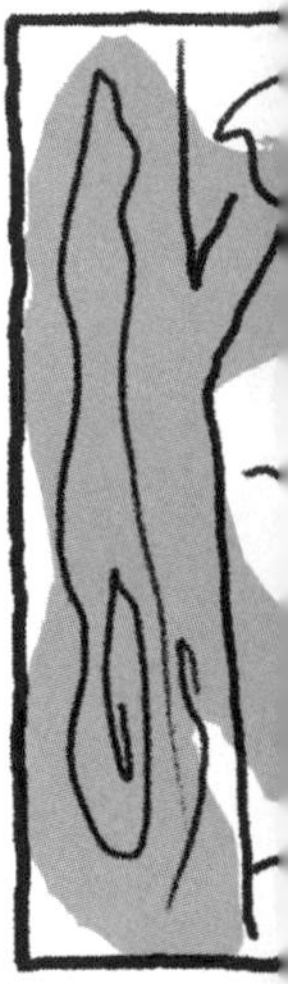

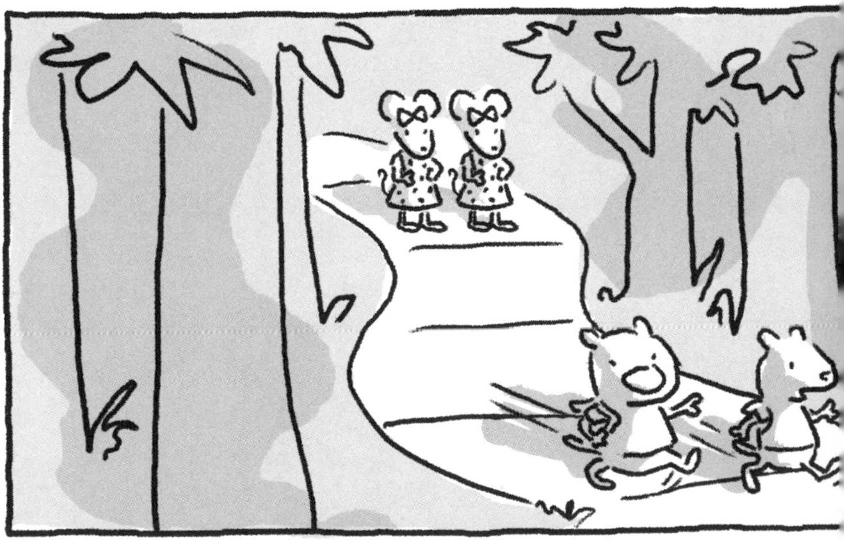

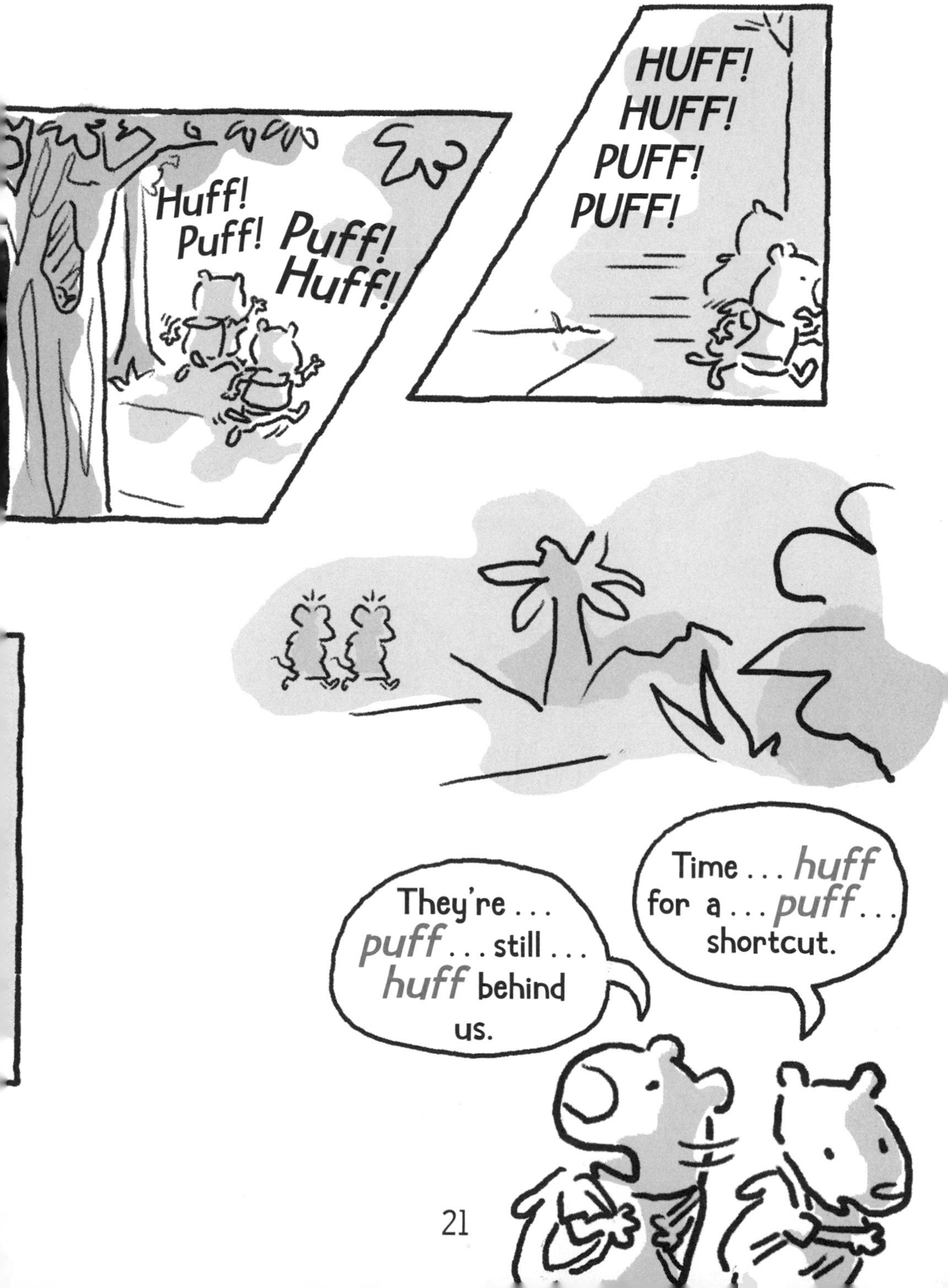
Huff! Puff! Puff! Huff!
HUFF! HUFF! PUFF! PUFF!
They're . . . *puff* . . . still . . . *huff* behind us.
Time . . . *huff* for a . . . *puff* . . . shortcut.

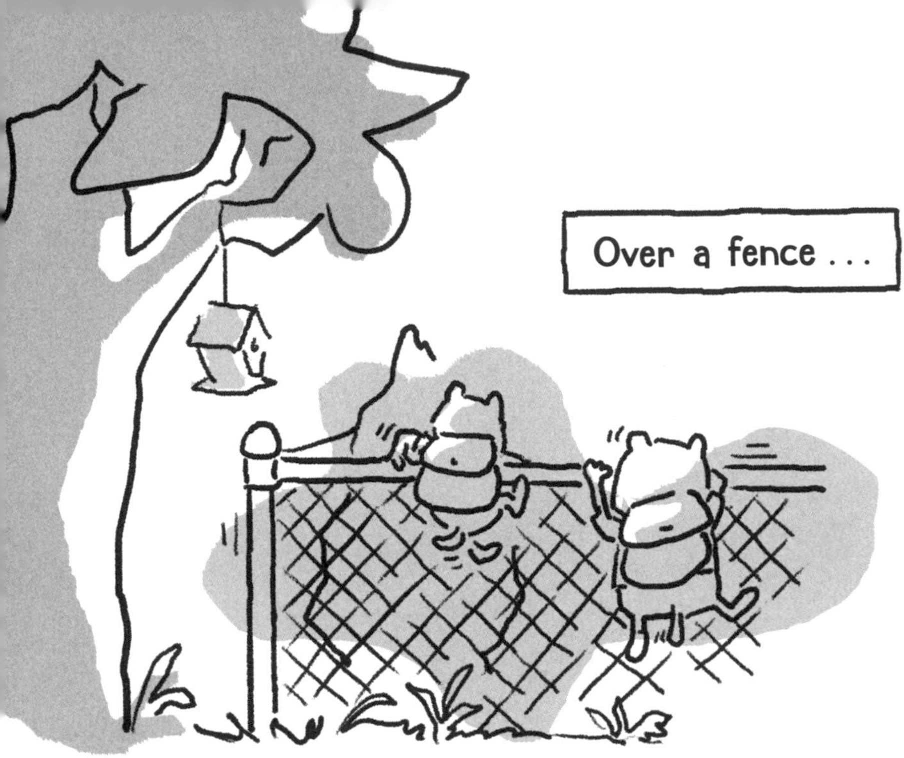
Over a fence . . .

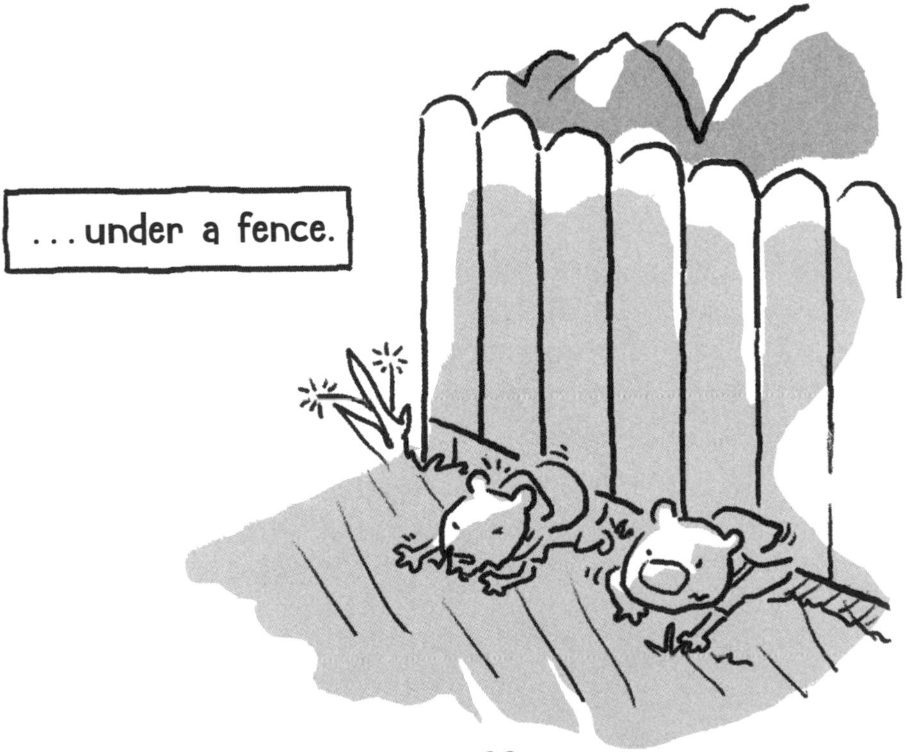
. . . under a fence.

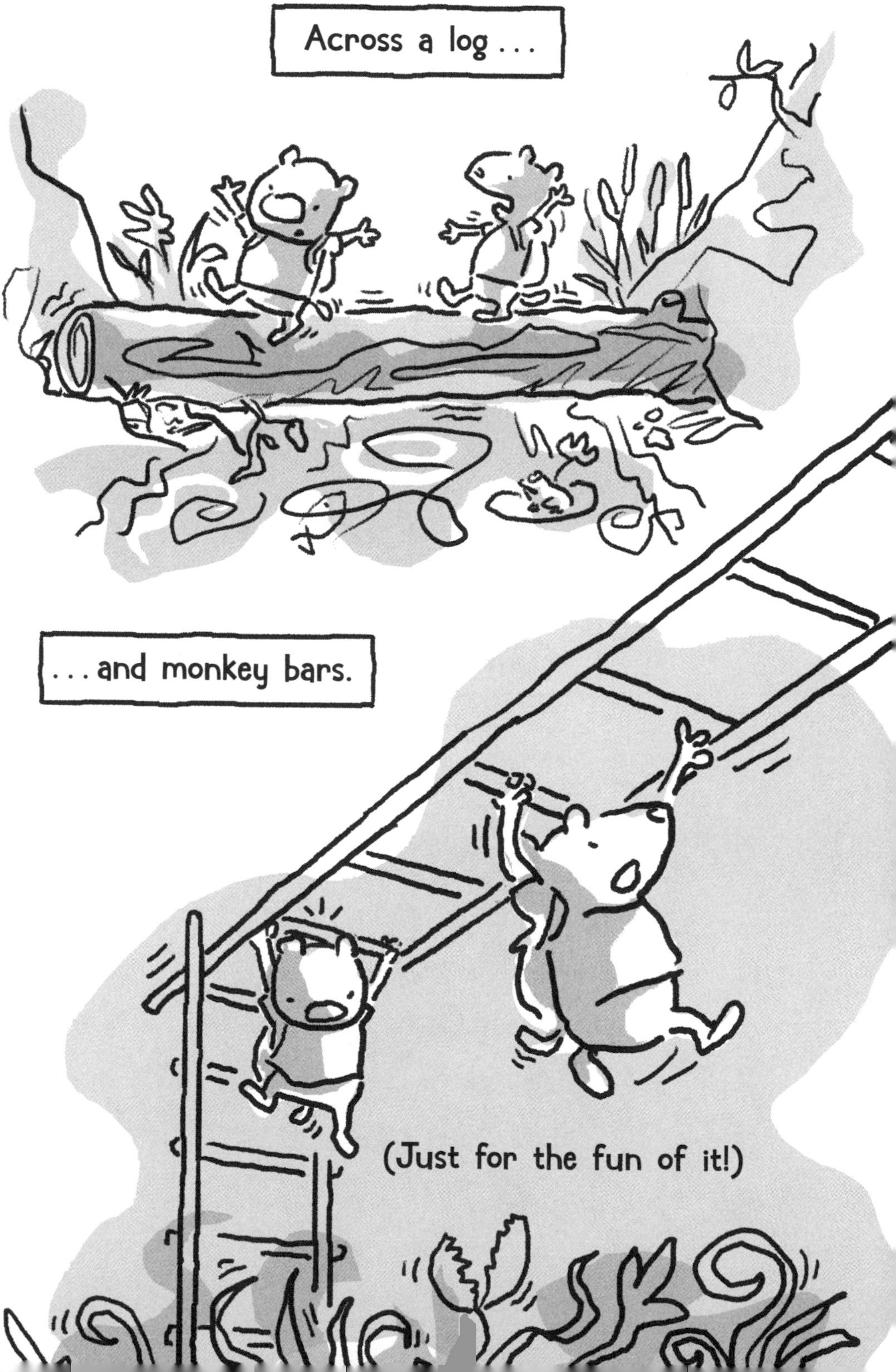
Across a log . . .
. . . and monkey bars.
(Just for the fun of it!)

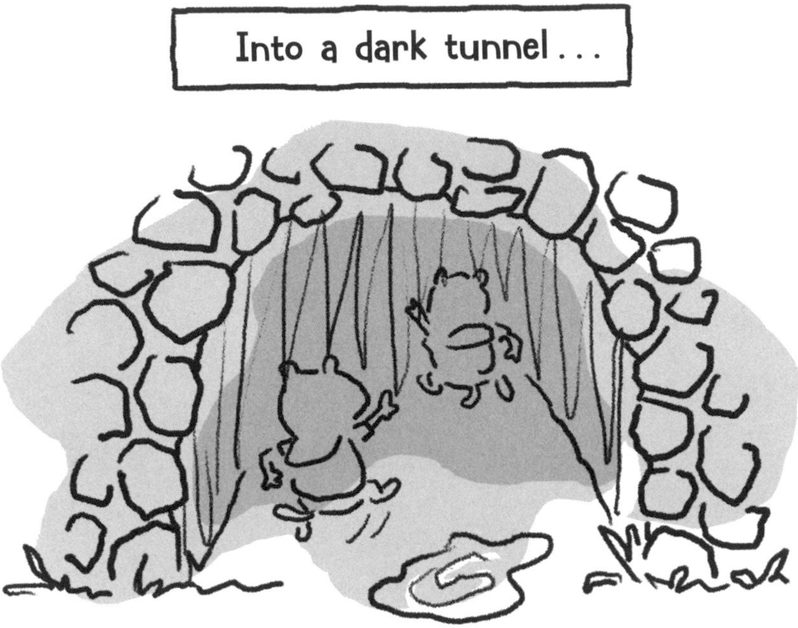
Into a dark tunnel . . .

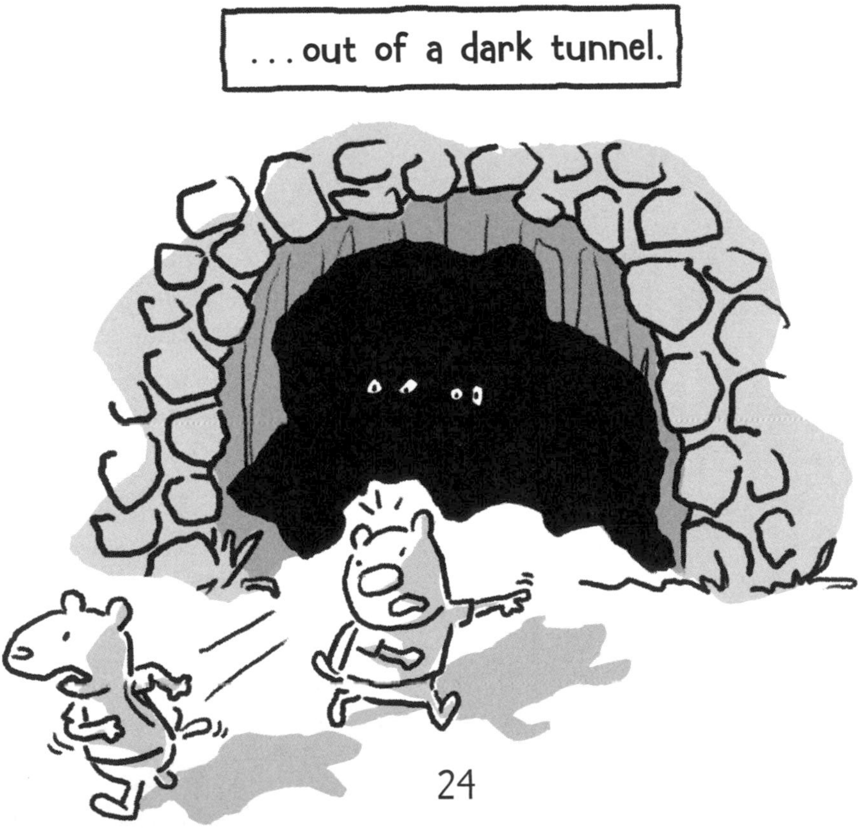
. . . out of a dark tunnel.

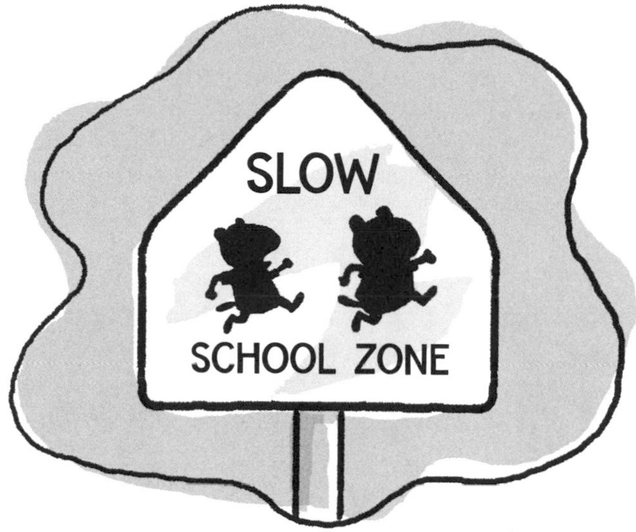
SLOW
SCHOOL ZONE

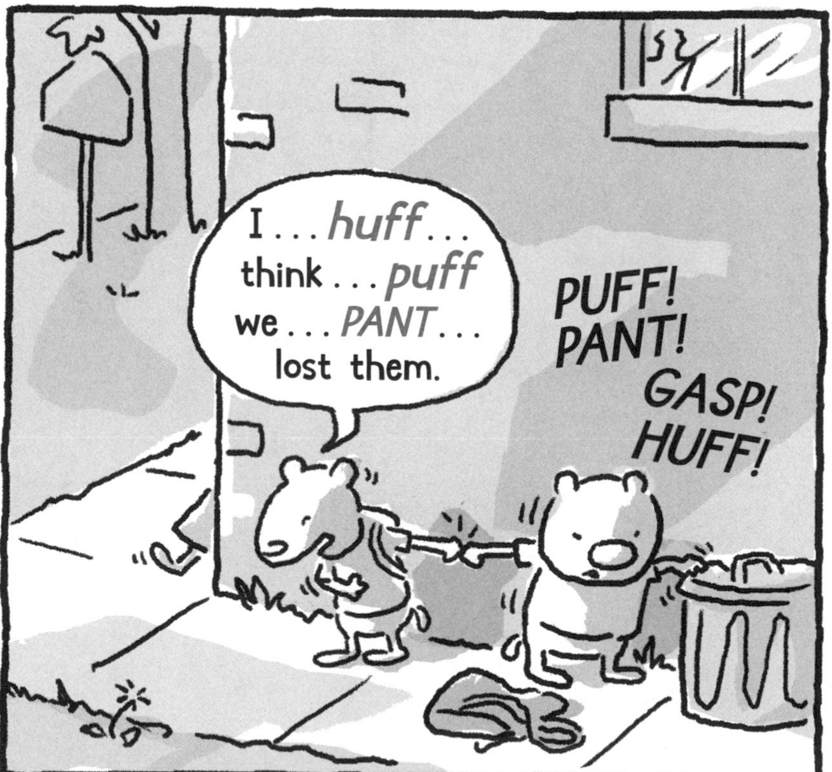
I . . . huff . . . think . . . puff we . . . PANT . . . lost them.
PUFF! PANT!
GASP! HUFF!

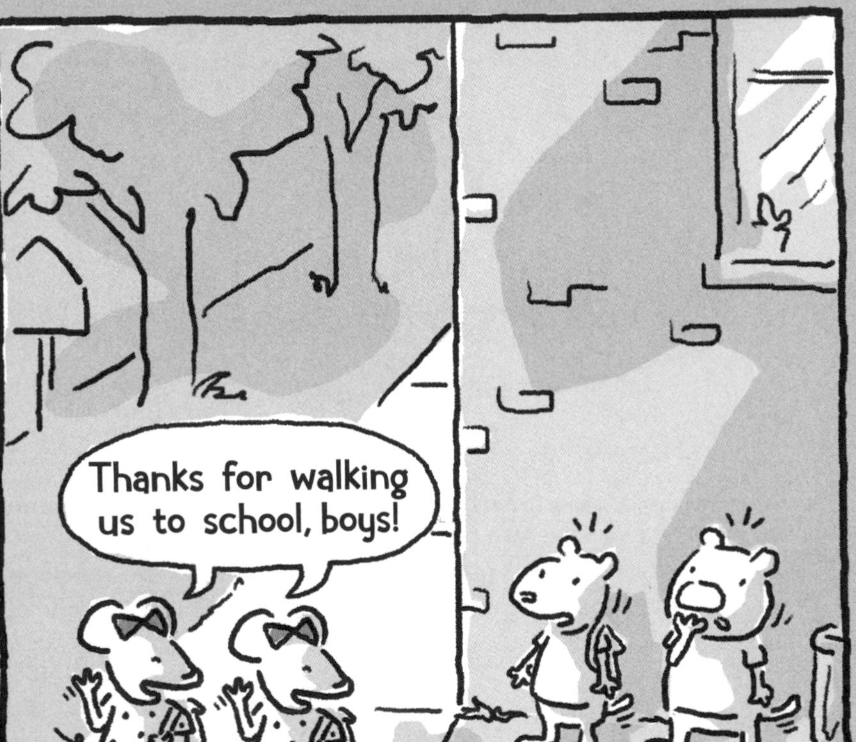
Thanks for walking us to school, boys!
OLD MACDONALD ELEMENTARY

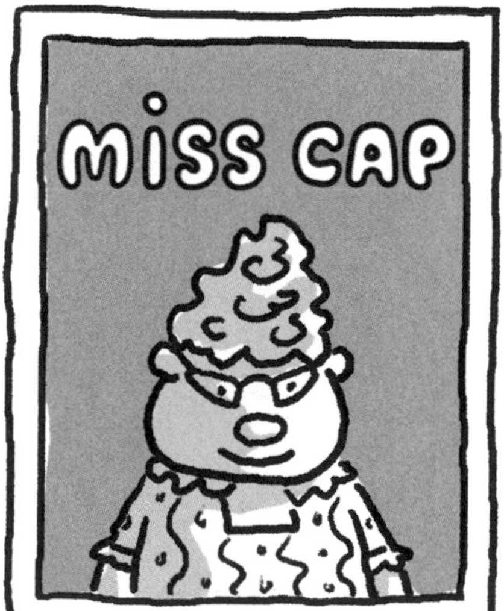
MISS CAP

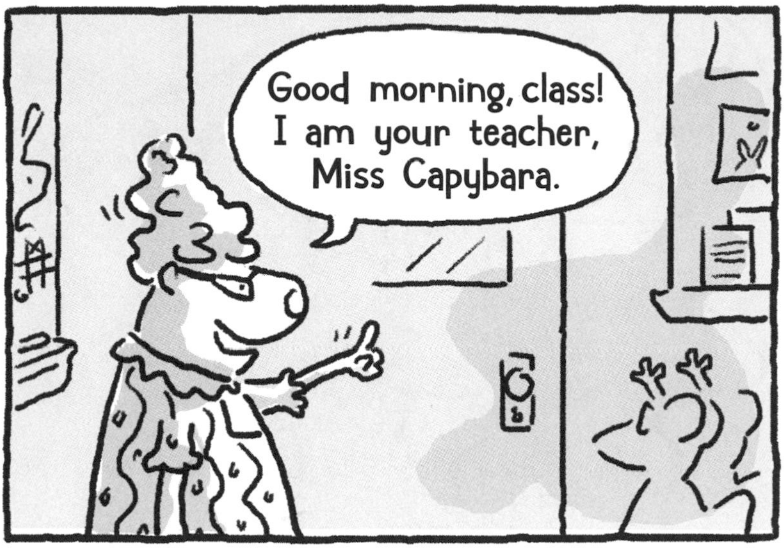
Good morning, class! I am your teacher, Miss Capybara.

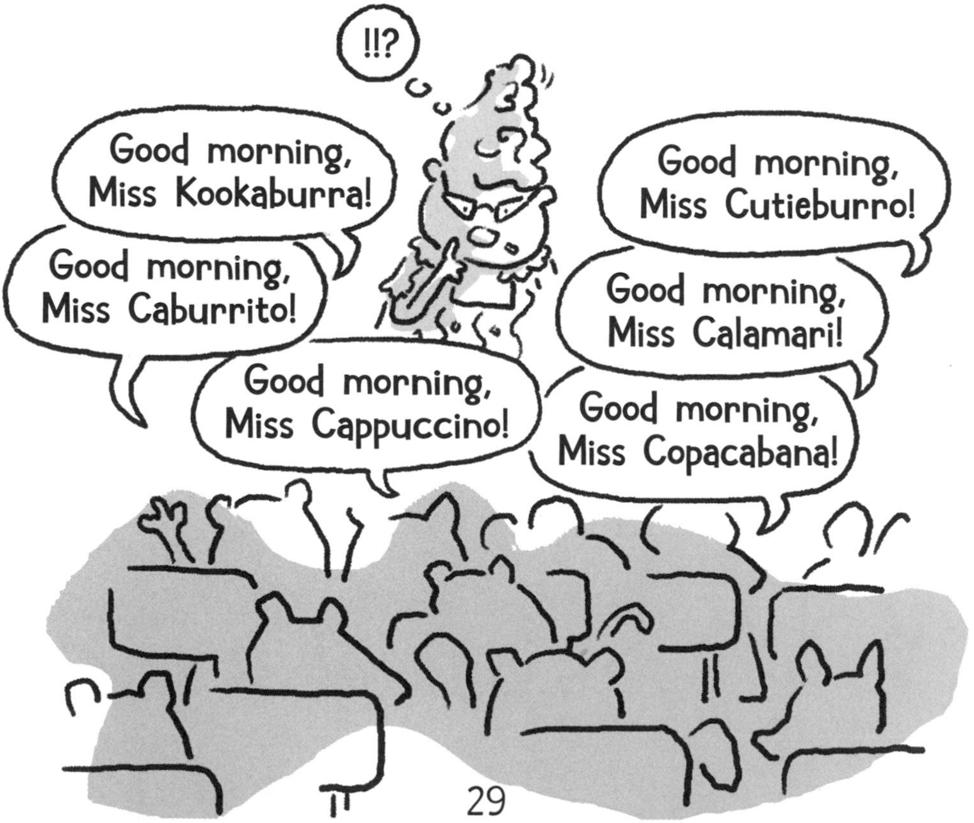
!!?
Good morning, Miss Kookaburra!
Good morning, Miss Caburrito!
Good morning, Miss Cappuccino!
Good morning, Miss Cutieburro!
Good morning, Miss Calamari!
Good morning, Miss Copacabana!

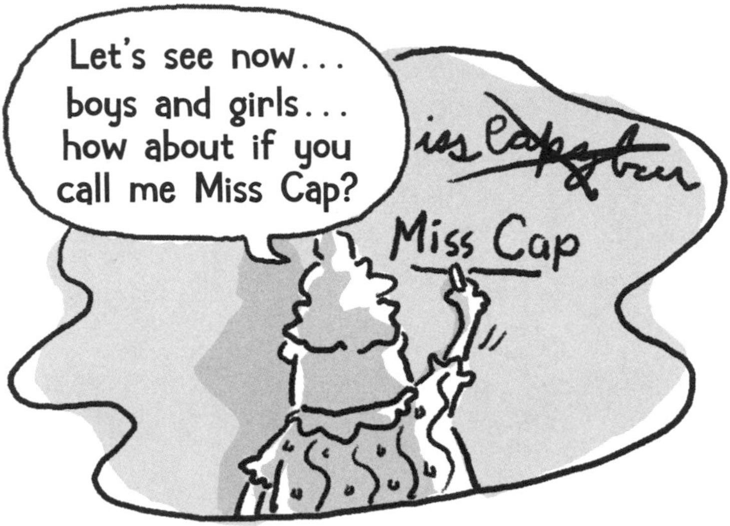
Let's see now... boys and girls... how about if you call me Miss Cap?
Miss Cap

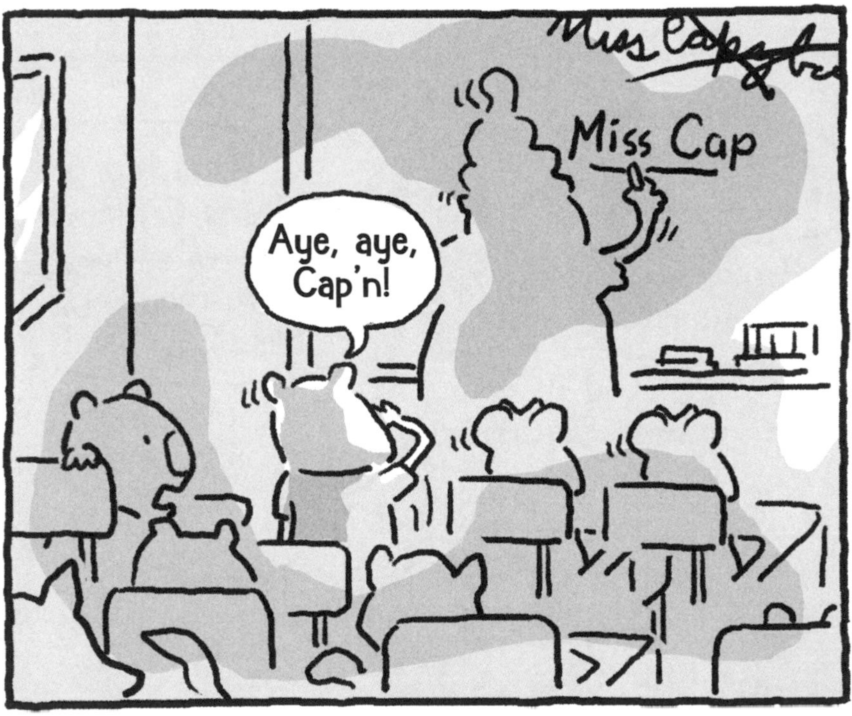
Miss Cap
Aye, aye, Cap'n!

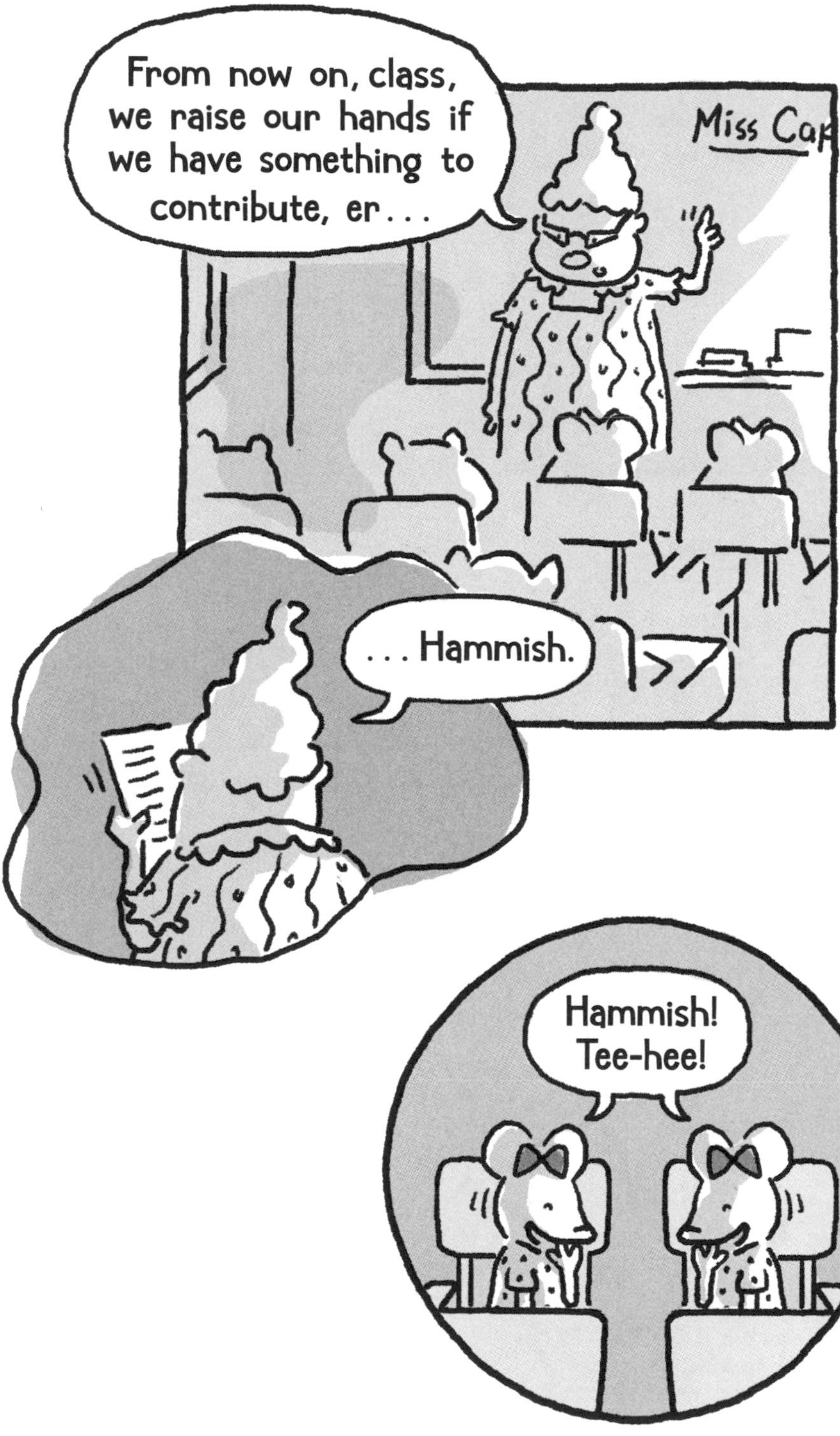
From now on, class, we raise our hands if we have something to contribute, er . . .
. . . Hammish.
Hammish! Tee-hee!

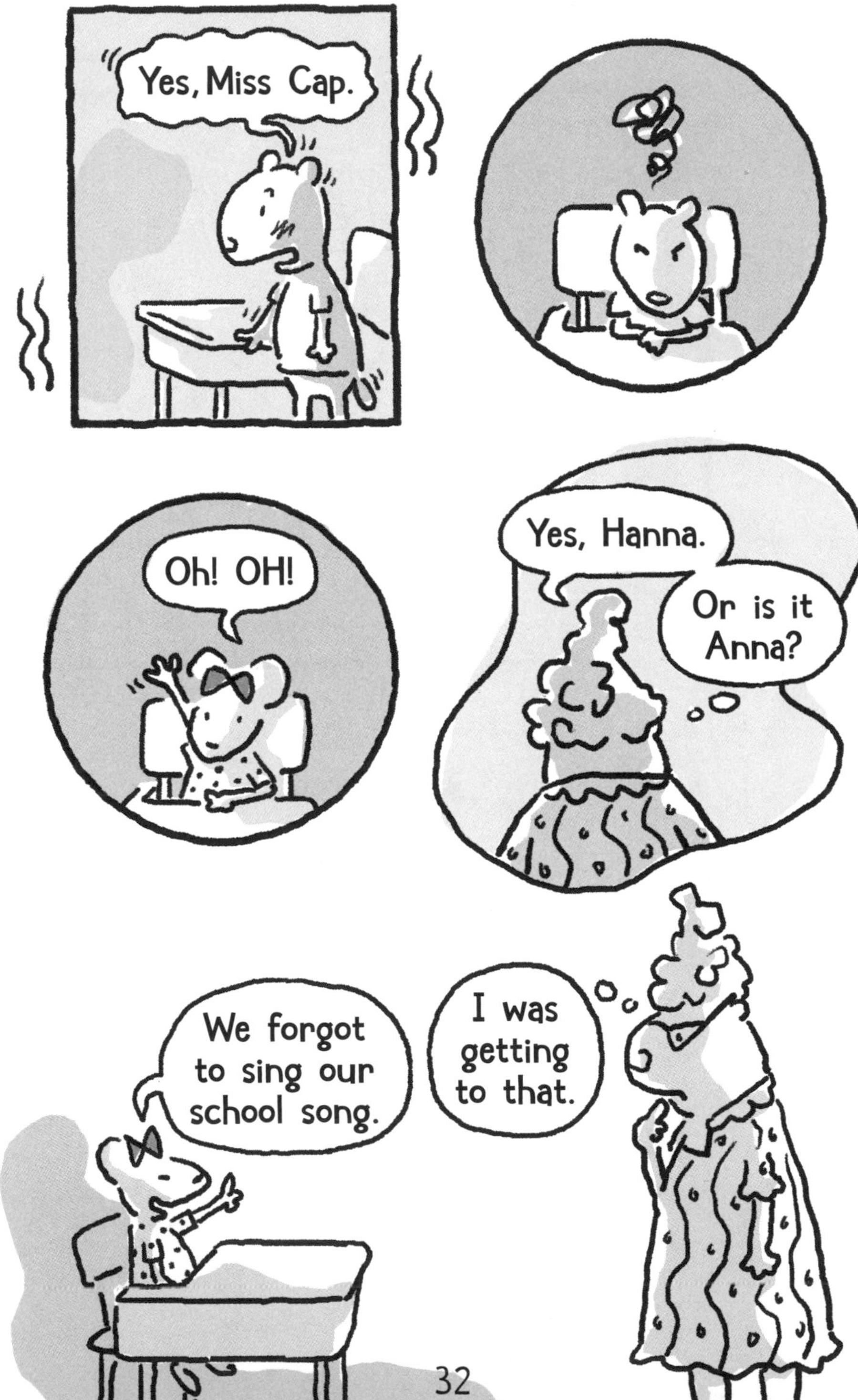
Yes, Miss Cap.
Oh! OH!
Yes, Hanna.
Or is it Anna?
We forgot to sing our school song.
I was getting to that.

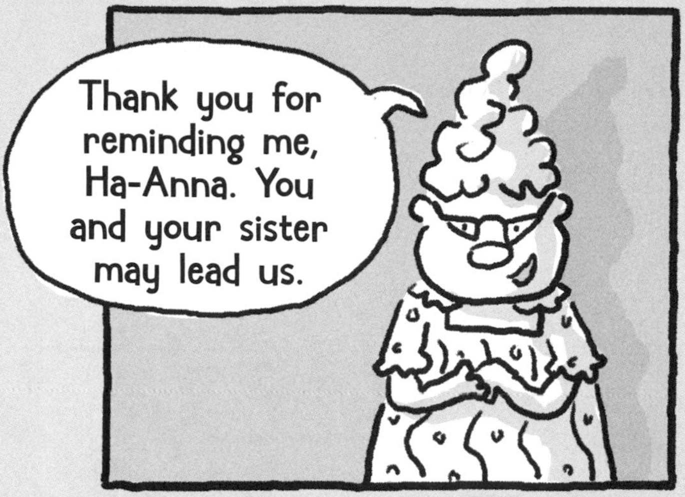
Thank you for reminding me, Ha-Anna. You and your sister may lead us.

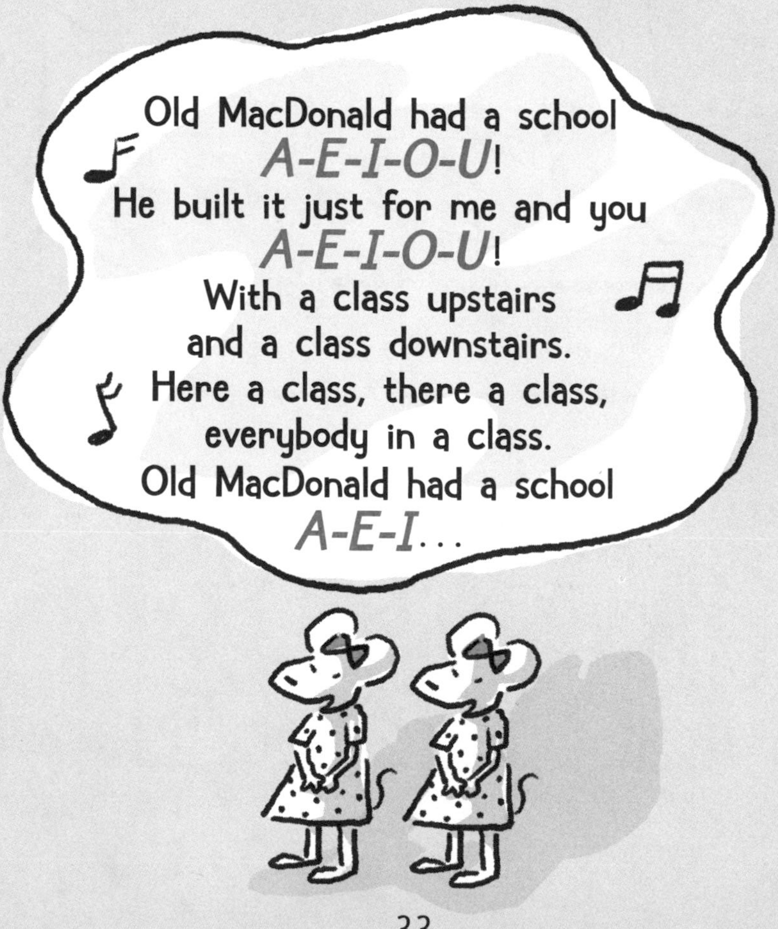
Old MacDonald had a school
A-E-I-O-U!
He built it just for me and you
A-E-I-O-U!
With a class upstairs
and a class downstairs.
Here a class, there a class,
everybody in a class.
Old MacDonald had a school
A-E-I...

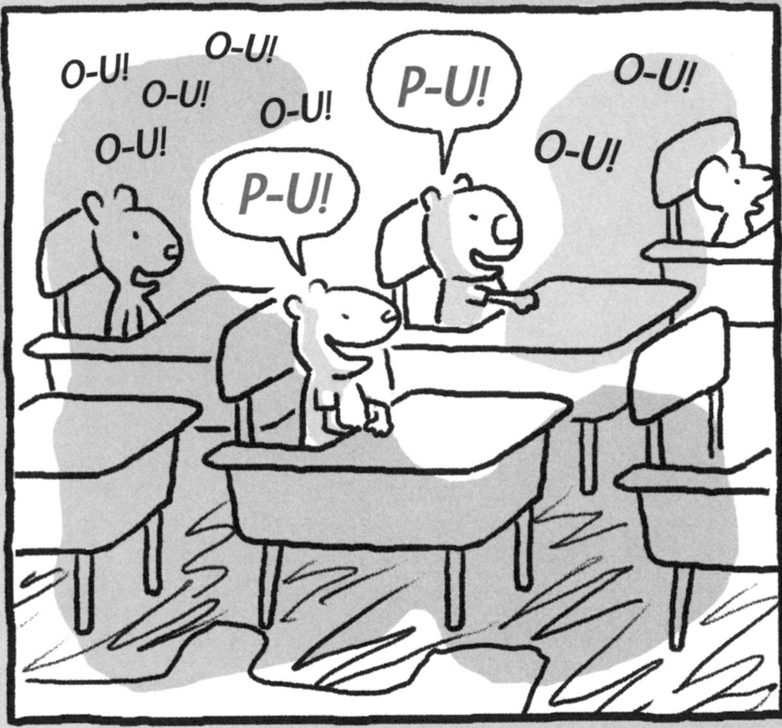
O-U!
O-U!
O-U!
O-U!
O-U!
P-U!
P-U!
O-U!
O-U!

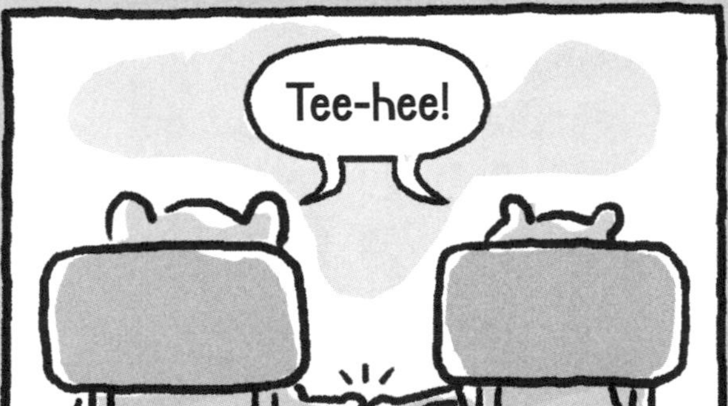
Tee-hee!

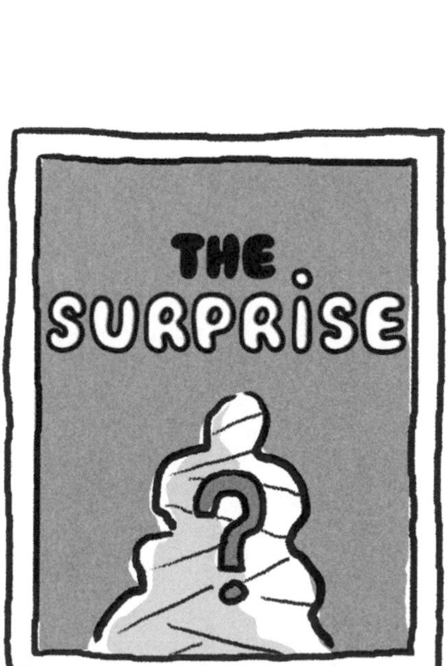
THE
SURPRISE

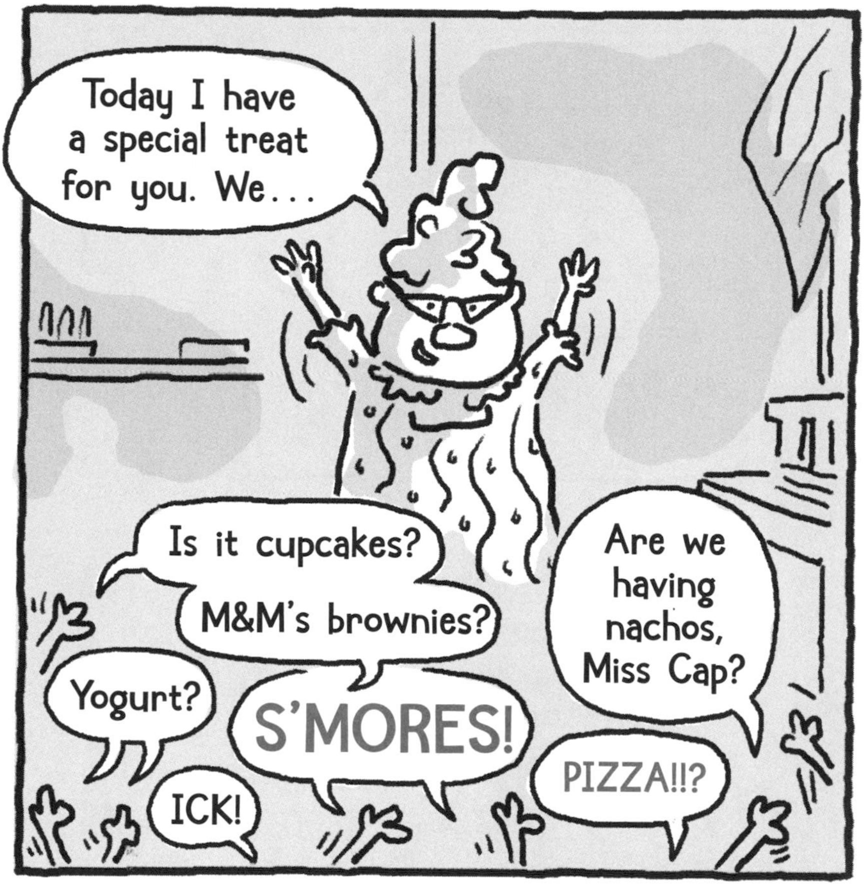
Today I have a special treat for you. We...
Is it cupcakes?
M&M's brownies?
Are we having nachos, Miss Cap?
Yogurt?
S'MORES!
PIZZA!!?
ICK!

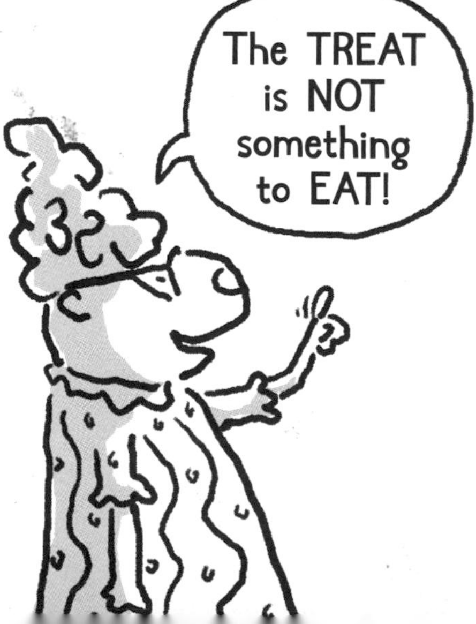
The TREAT is NOT something to EAT!

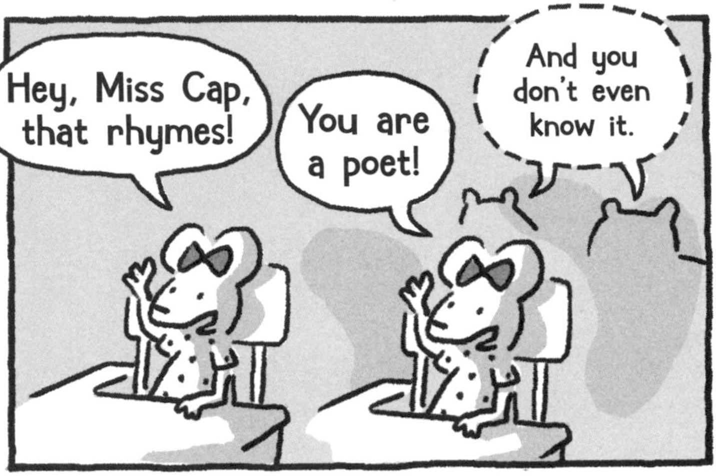
Hey, Miss Cap, that rhymes!
You are a poet!
And you don't even know it.

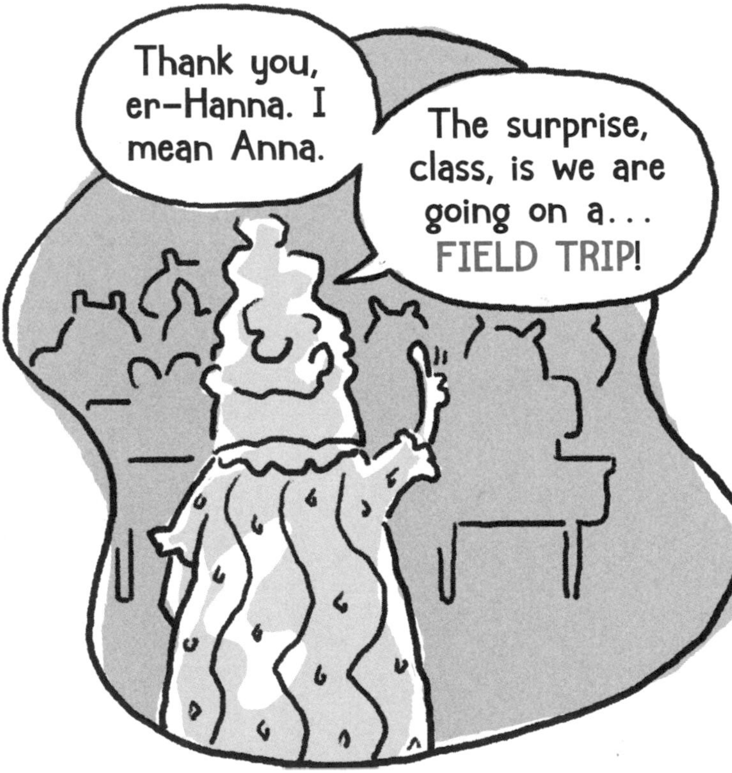
Thank you, er–Hanna. I mean Anna.
The surprise, class, is we are going on a... FIELD TRIP!

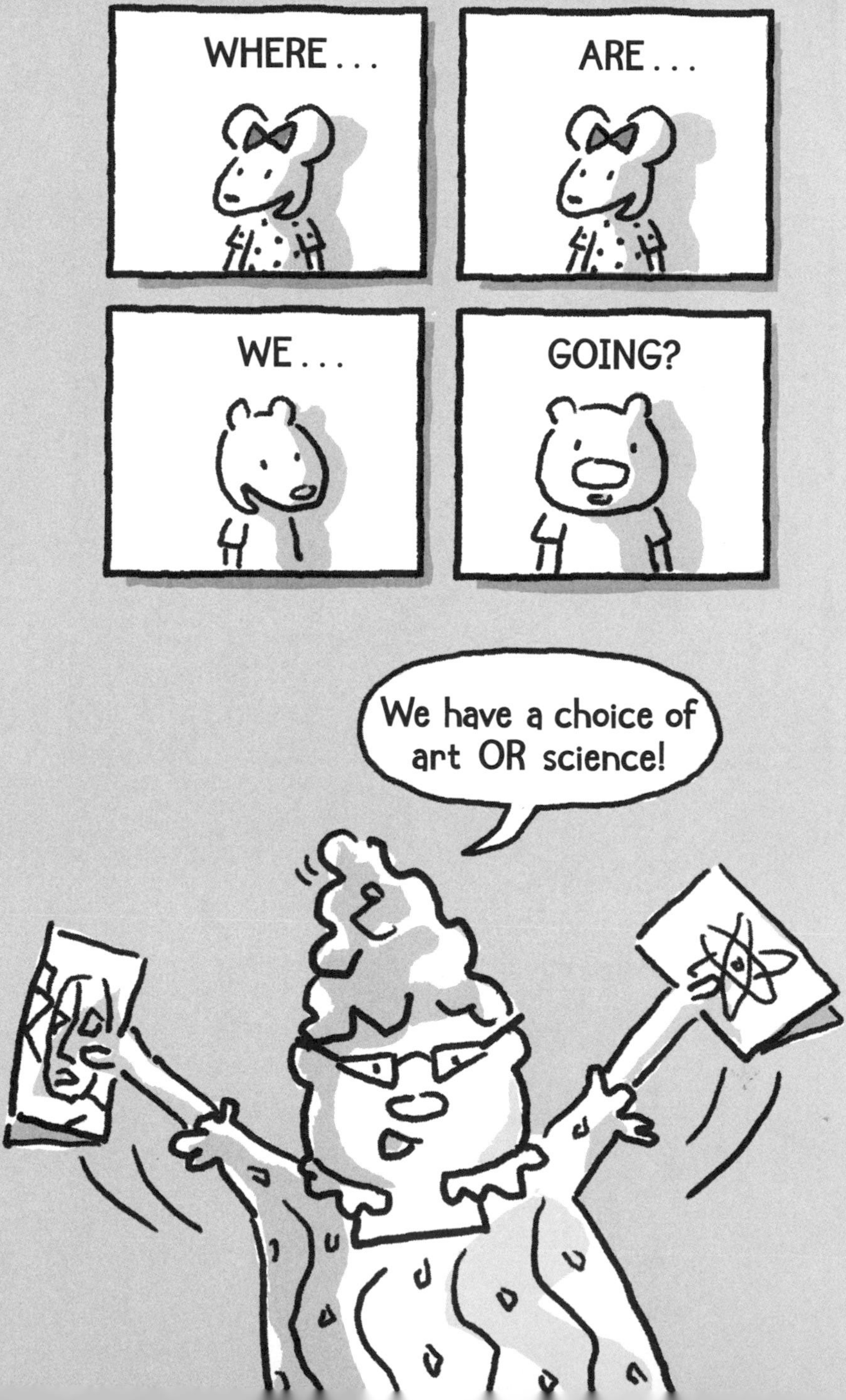
WHERE...
ARE...
WE...
GOING?
We have a choice of art OR science!

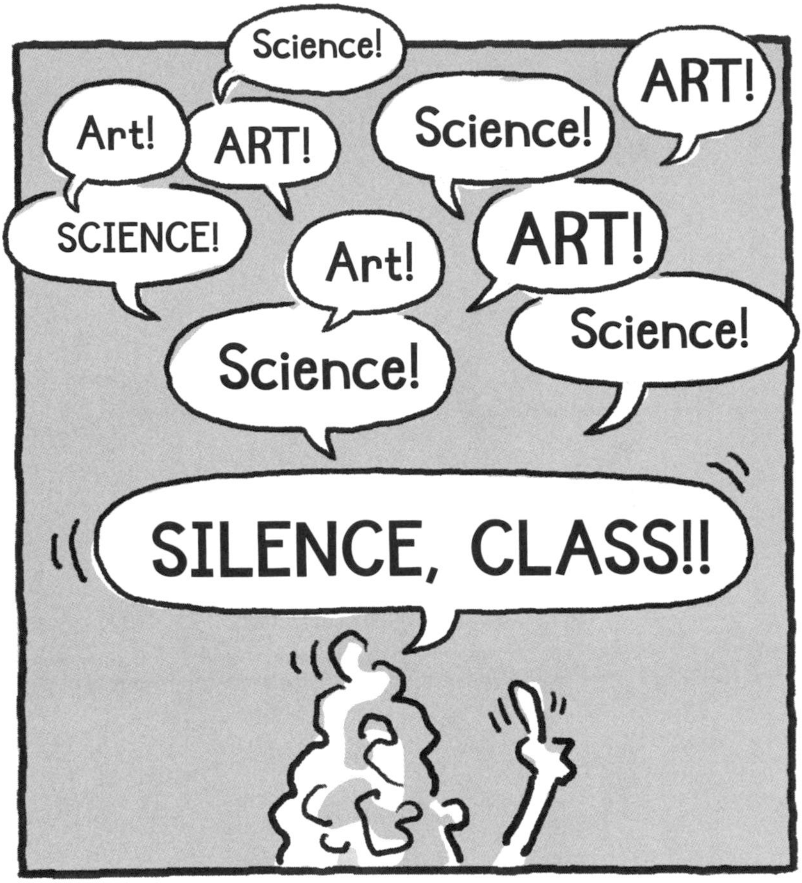
Science!
Art!
ART!
Science!
ART!
SCIENCE!
Art!
ART!
Science!
Science!
SILENCE, CLASS!!

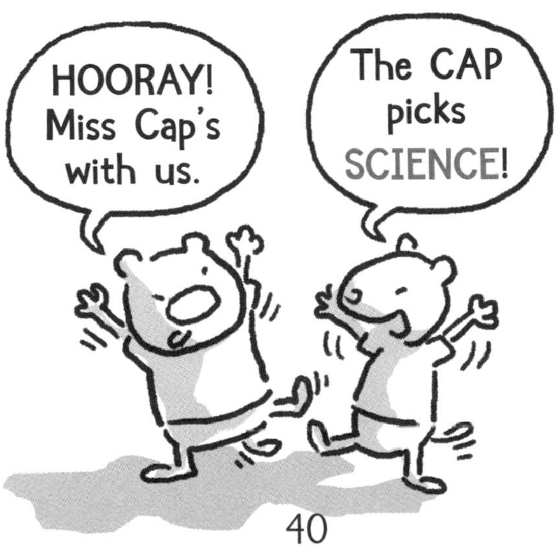
HOORAY! Miss Cap's with us.
The CAP picks SCIENCE!

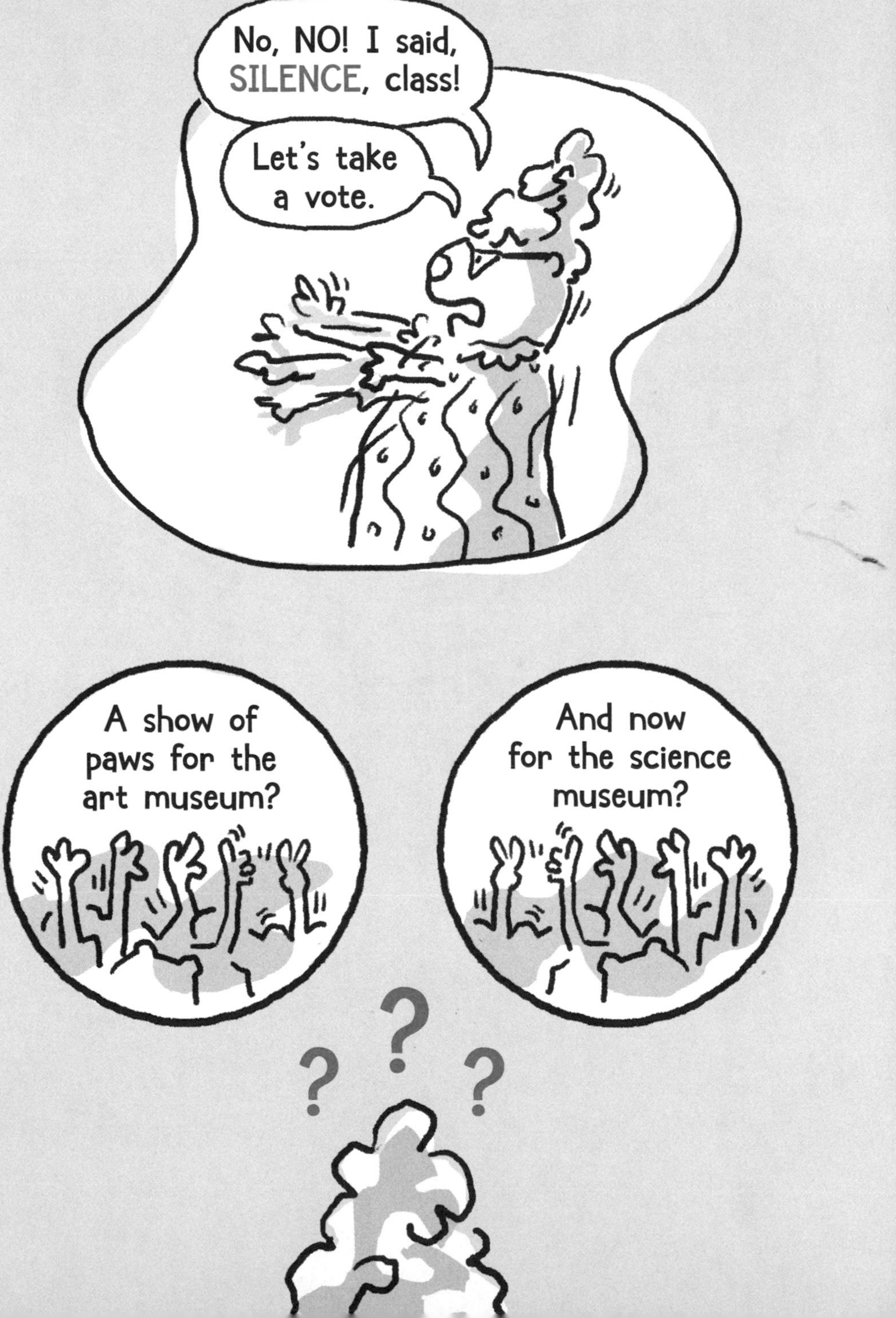

No, NO! I said, SILENCE, class!
Let's take a vote.
A show of paws for the art museum?
And now for the science museum?
? ? ?

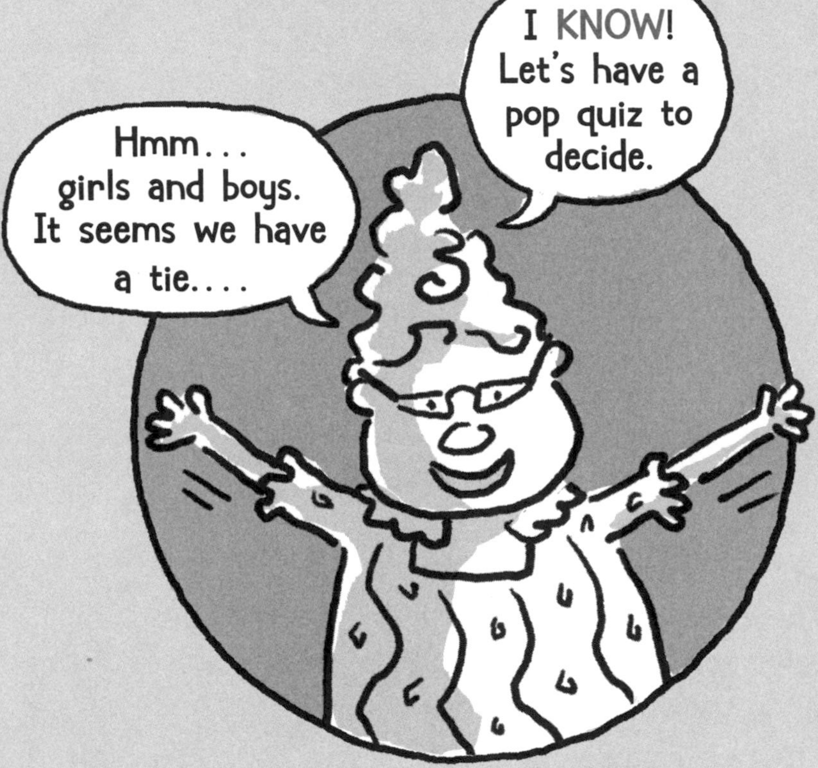
Hmm... girls and boys. It seems we have a tie....
I KNOW! Let's have a pop quiz to decide.

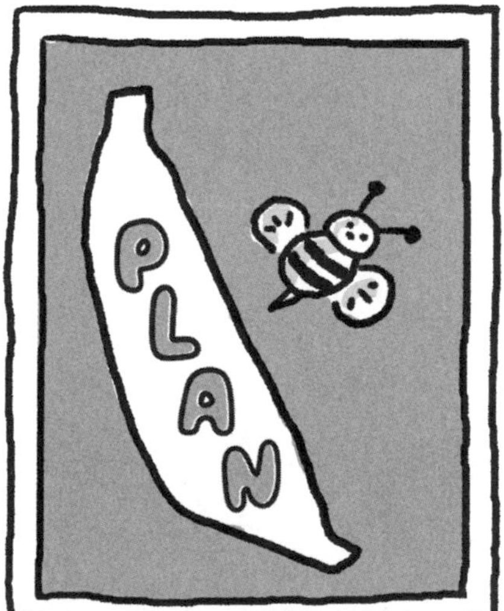
PLAN

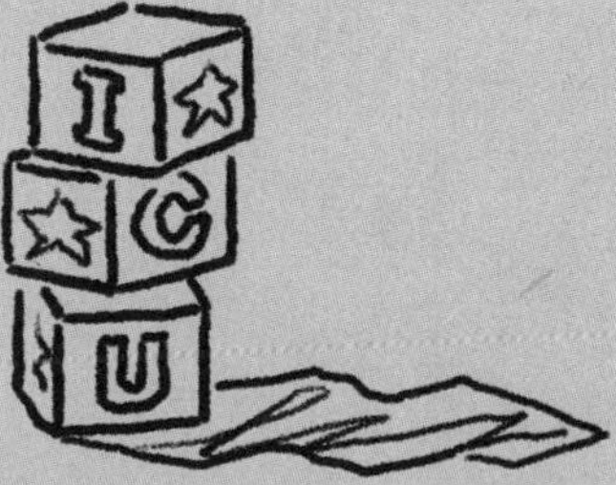
I
C
U

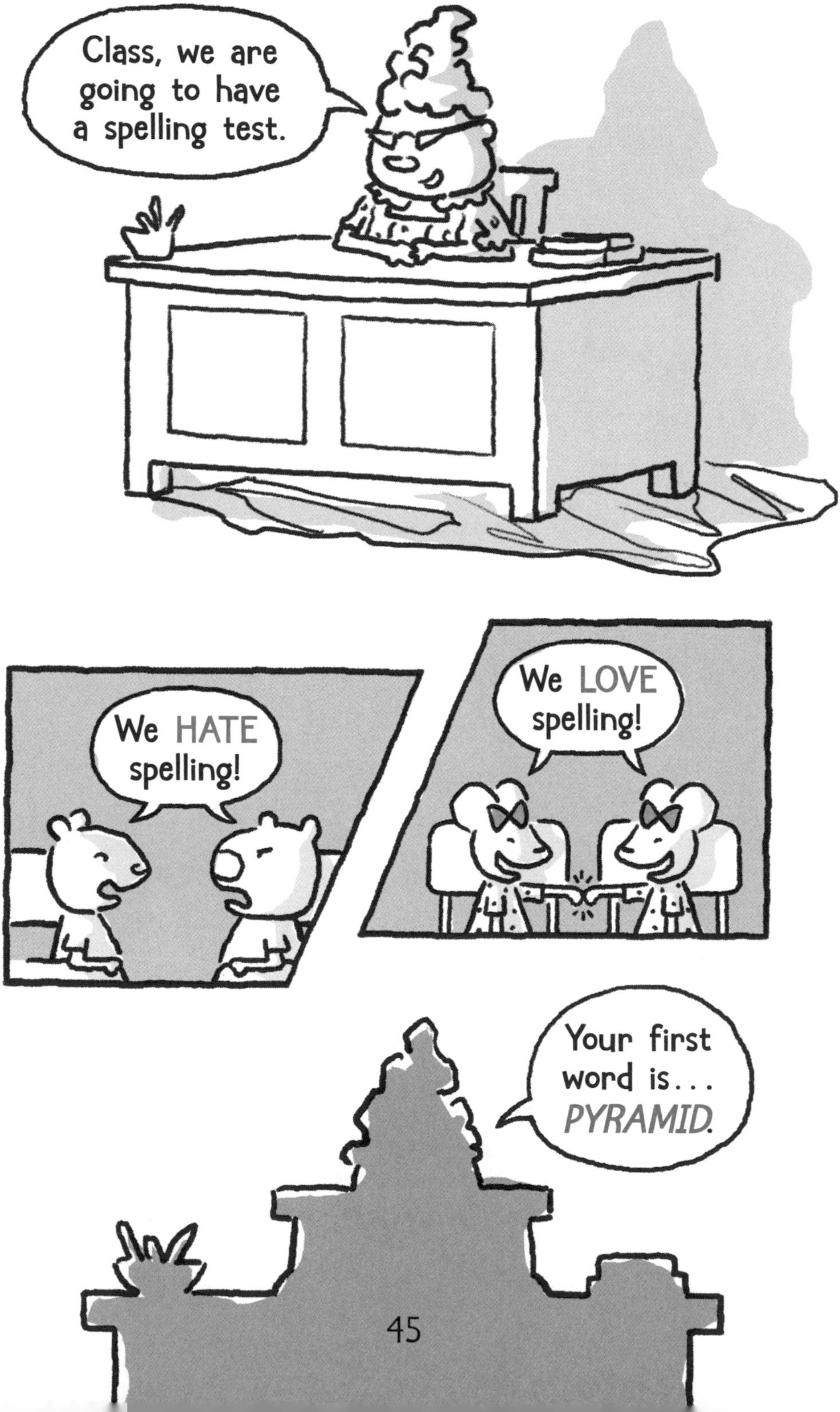
Class, we are going to have a spelling test.
We HATE spelling!
We LOVE spelling!
Your first word is... PYRAMID.

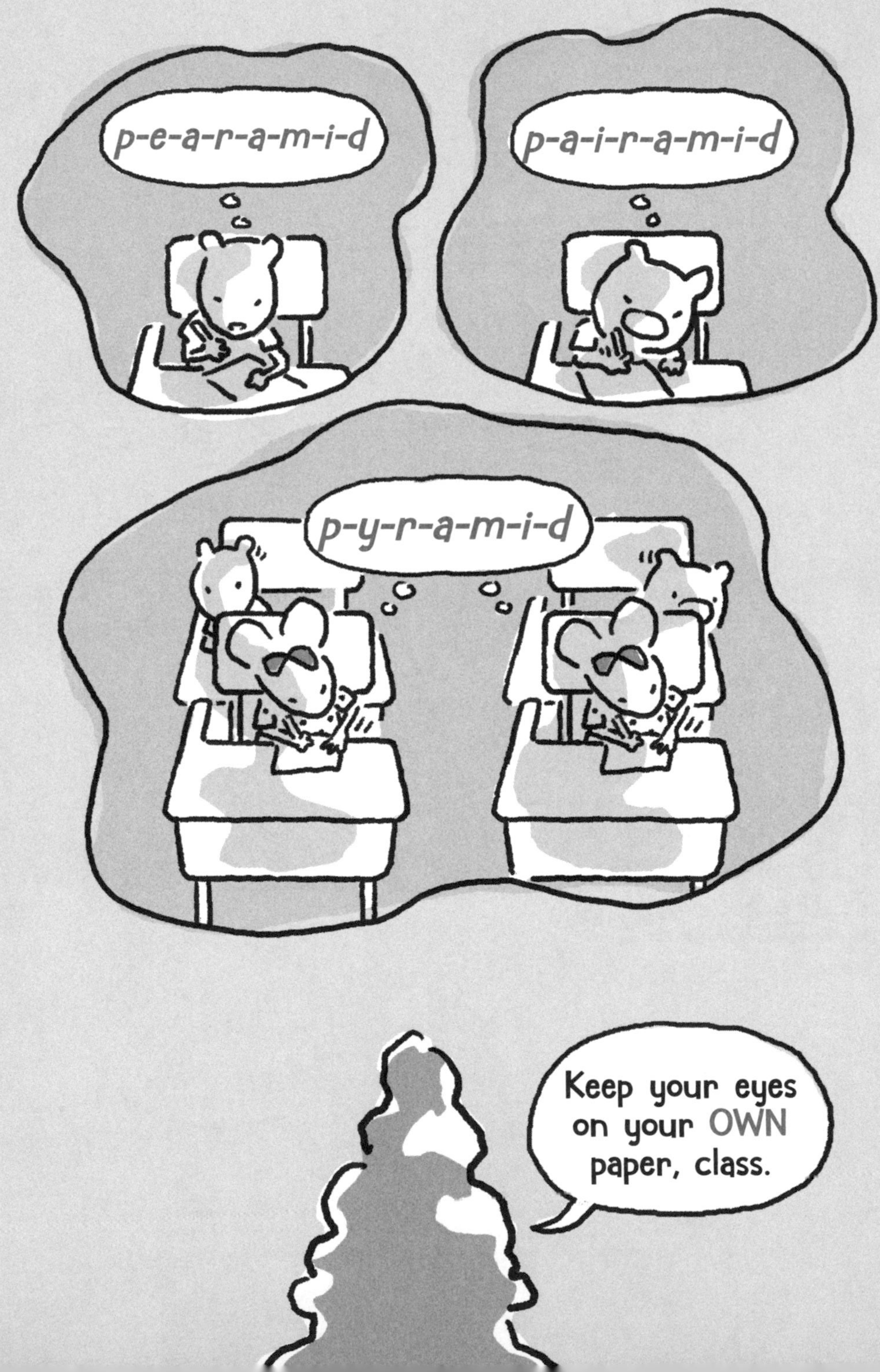
p-e-a-r-a-m-i-d
p-a-i-r-a-m-i-d
p-y-r-a-m-i-d
Keep your eyes on your OWN paper, class.

Time's up. Please pass your papers to the front.

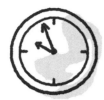

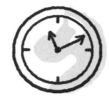

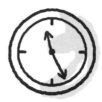

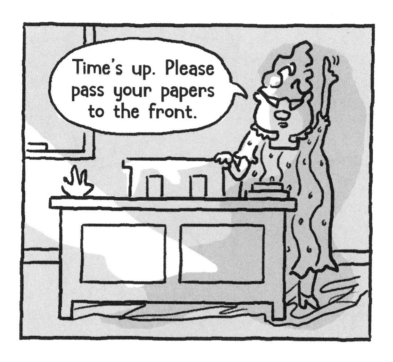

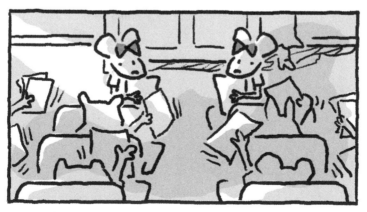

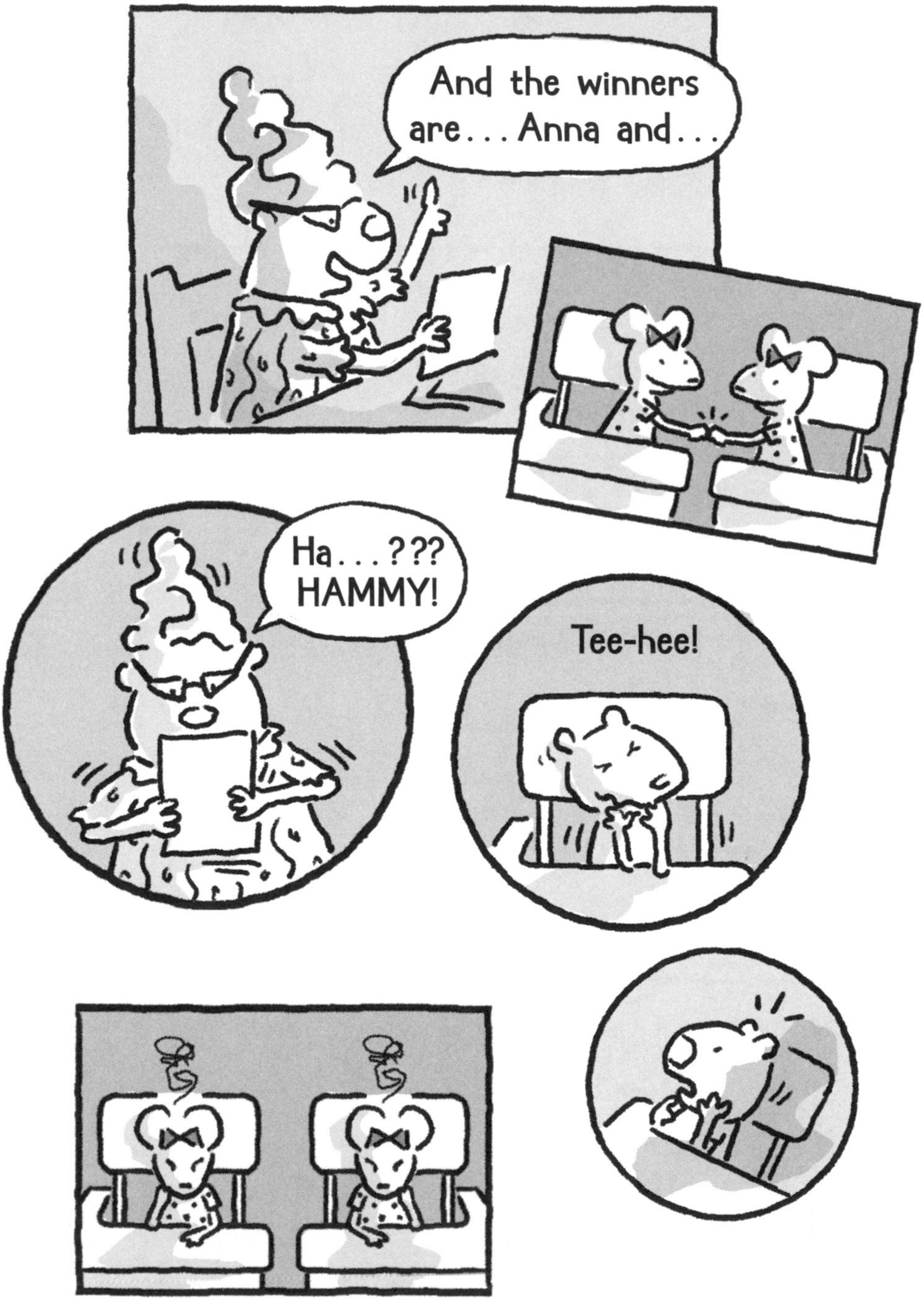
And the winners are. . . Anna and. . .
Ha. . . ??? HAMMY!
Tee-hee!

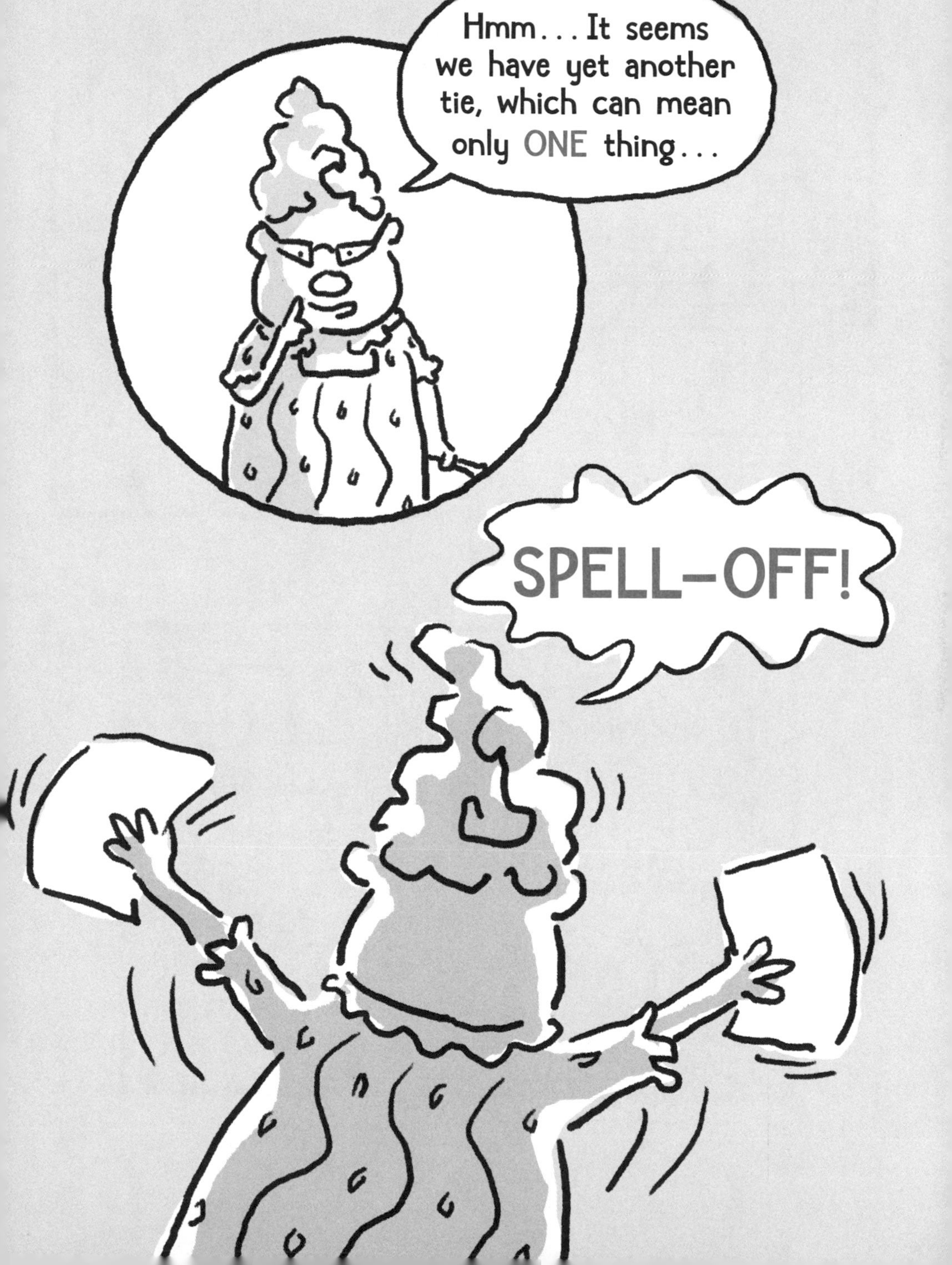
Hmm... It seems we have yet another tie, which can mean only ONE thing...
SPELL-OFF!

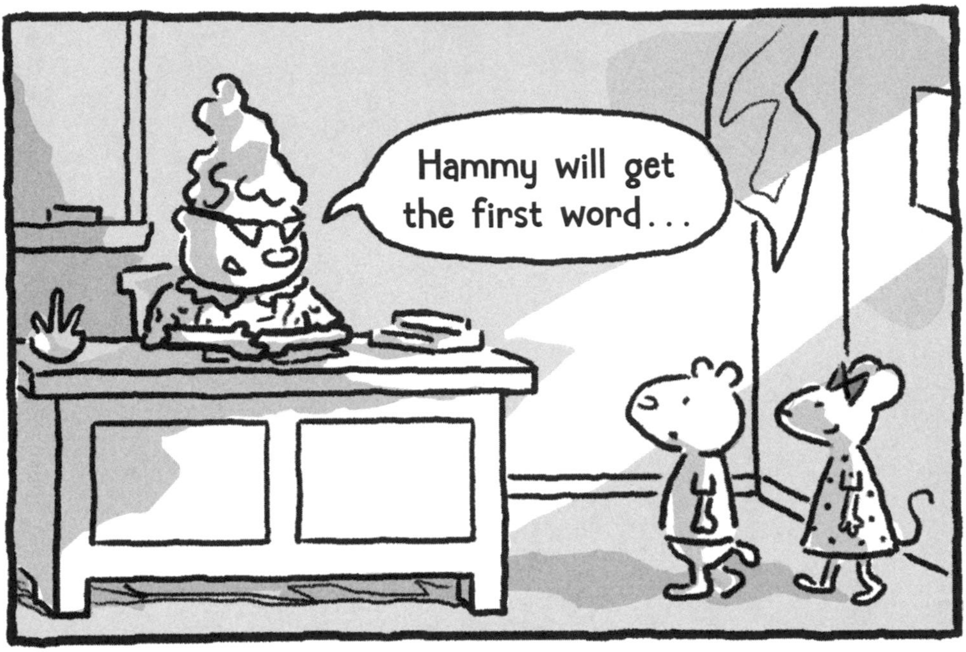
Hammy will get the first word...

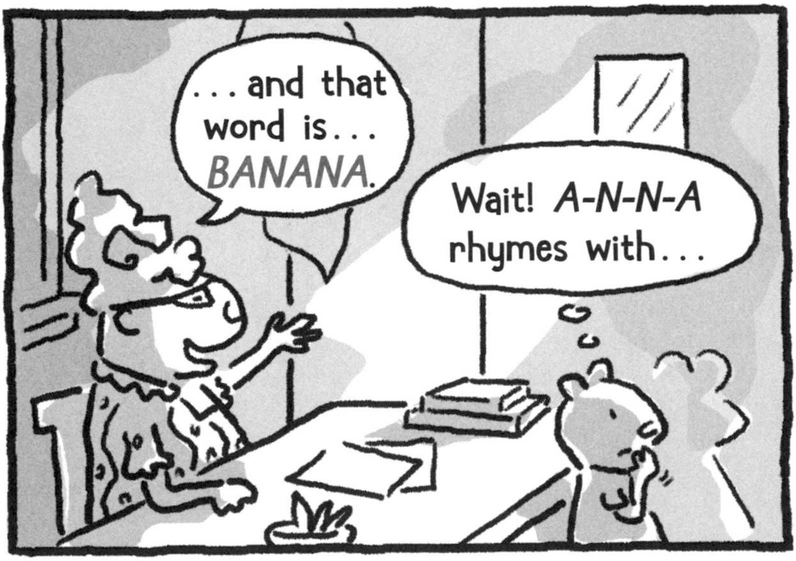
...and that word is... *BANANA*.
Wait! *A-N-N-A* rhymes with...

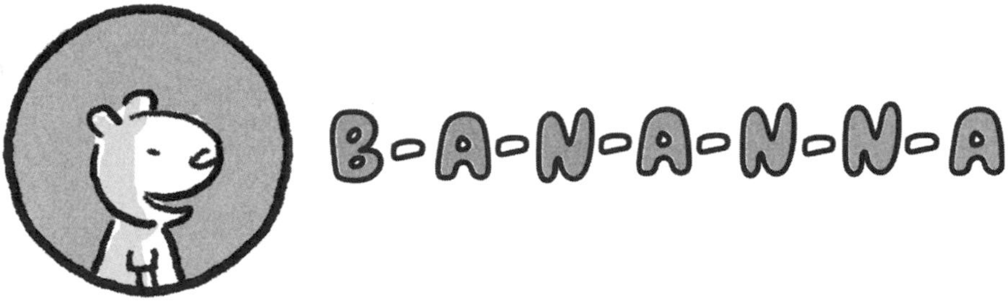
B-A-N-A-N-N-A

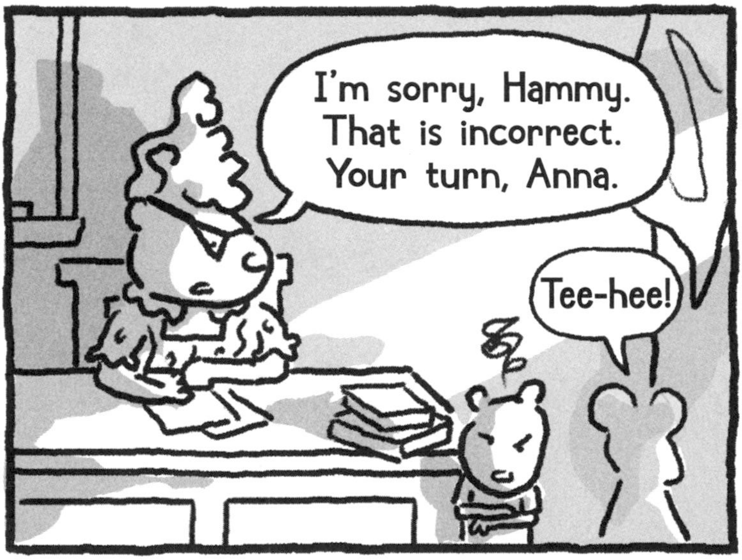
I'm sorry, Hammy. That is incorrect. Your turn, Anna.
Tee-hee!

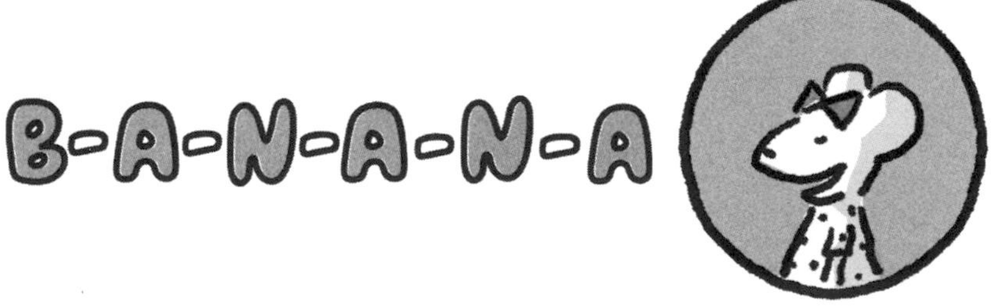
B-A-N-A-N-A

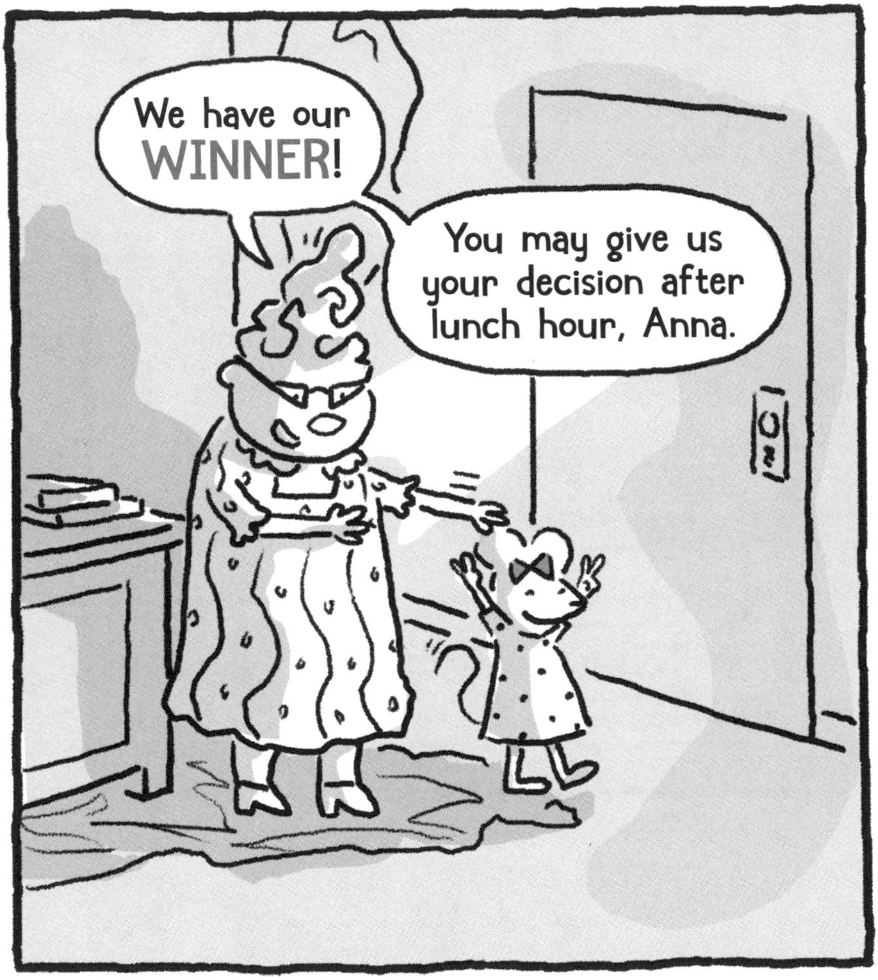
We have our WINNER!
You may give us your decision after lunch hour, Anna.

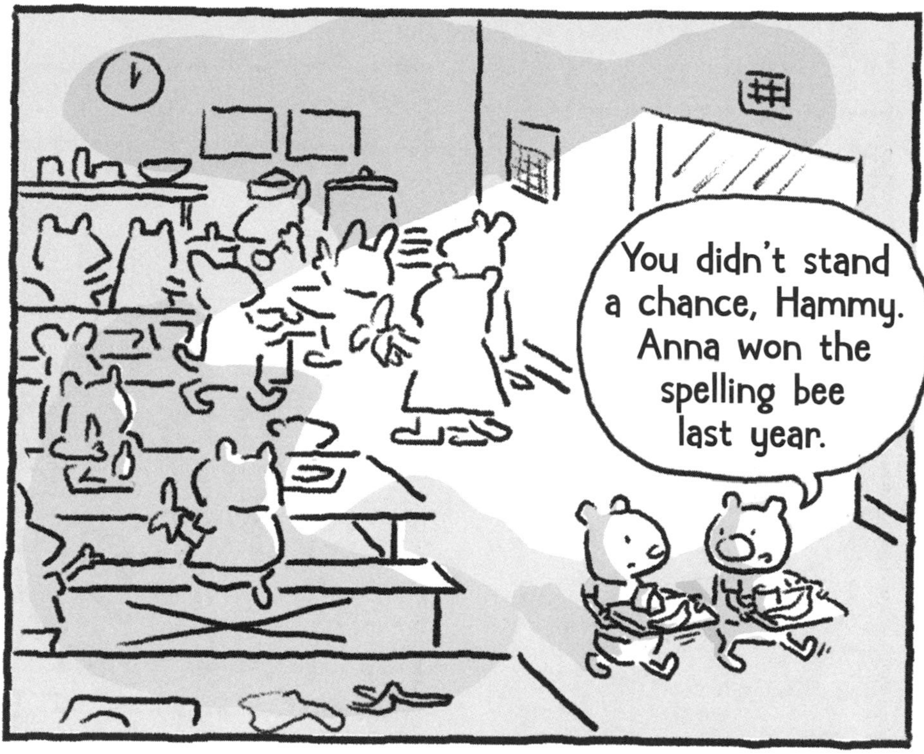
You didn't stand a chance, Hammy. Anna won the spelling bee last year.

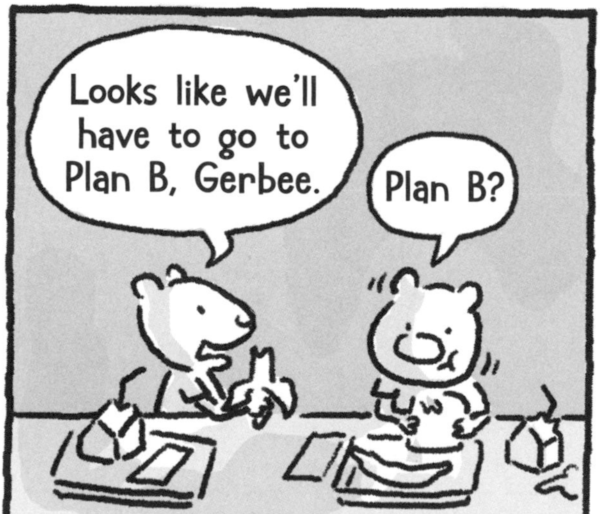
Looks like we'll have to go to Plan B, Gerbee.
Plan B?

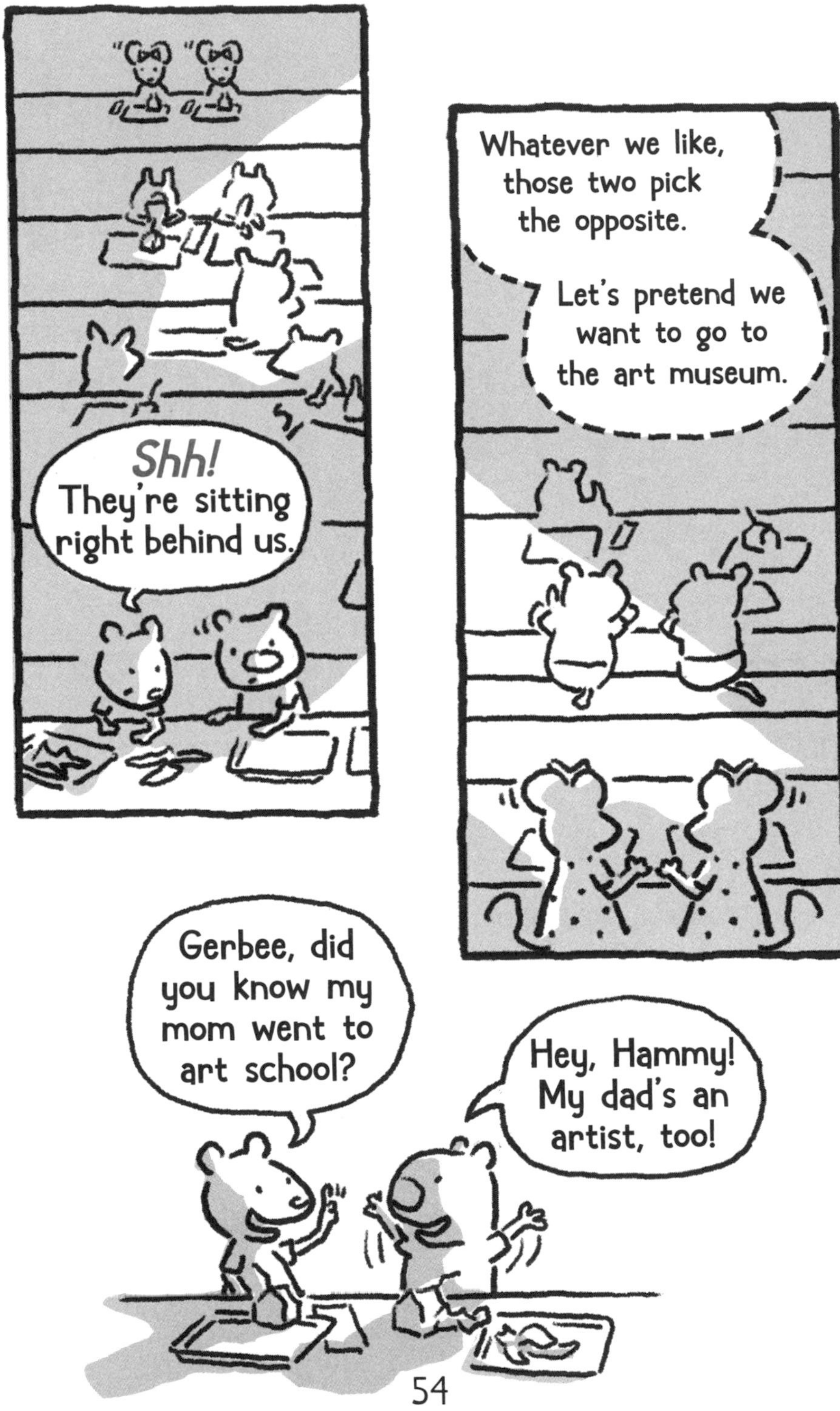
Shh! They're sitting right behind us.
Whatever we like, those two pick the opposite.
Let's pretend we want to go to the art museum.
Gerbee, did you know my mom went to art school?
Hey, Hammy! My dad's an artist, too!

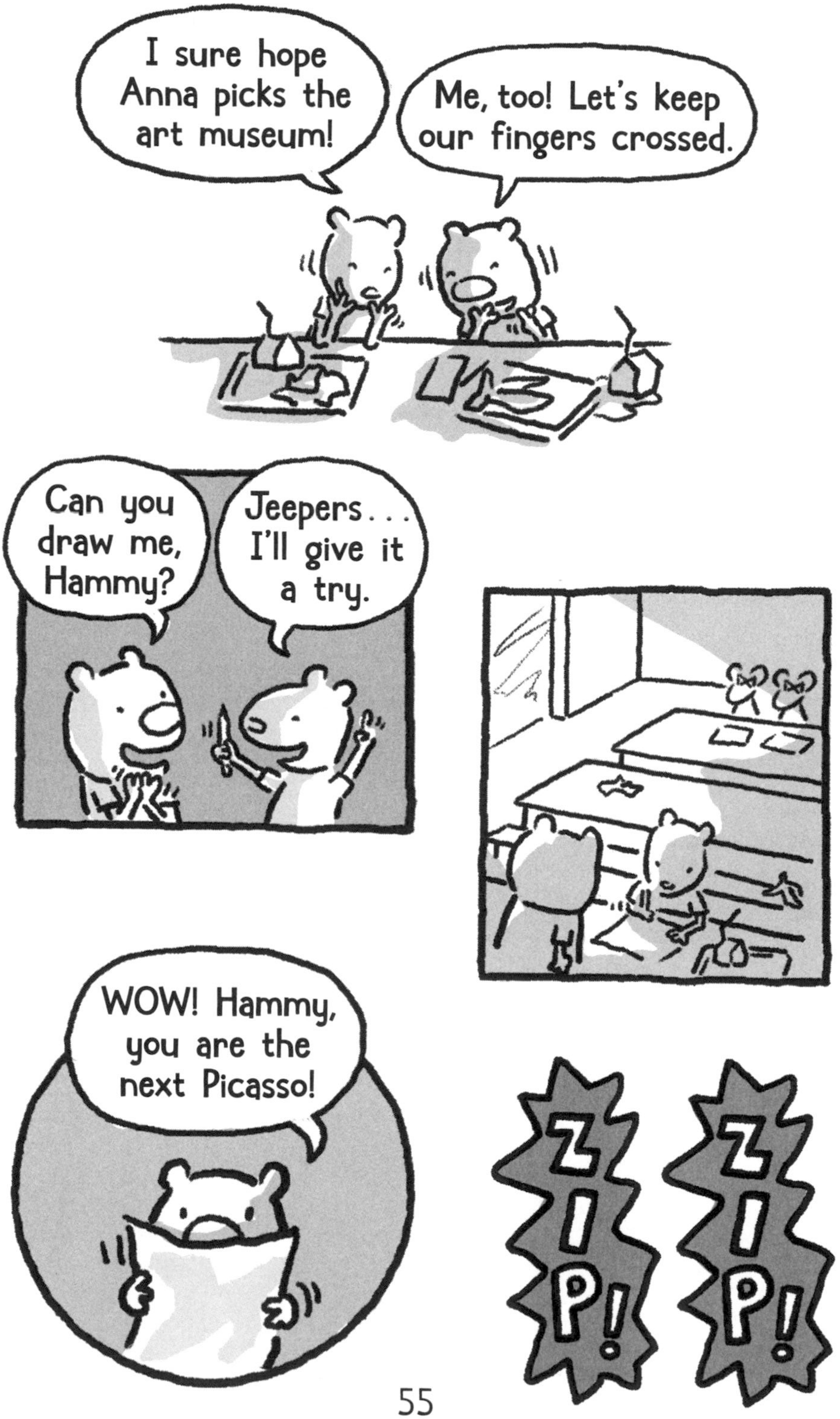
I sure hope Anna picks the art museum!
Me, too! Let's keep our fingers crossed.
Can you draw me, Hammy?
Jeepers... I'll give it a try.
WOW! Hammy, you are the next Picasso!
ZIP!
ZIP!

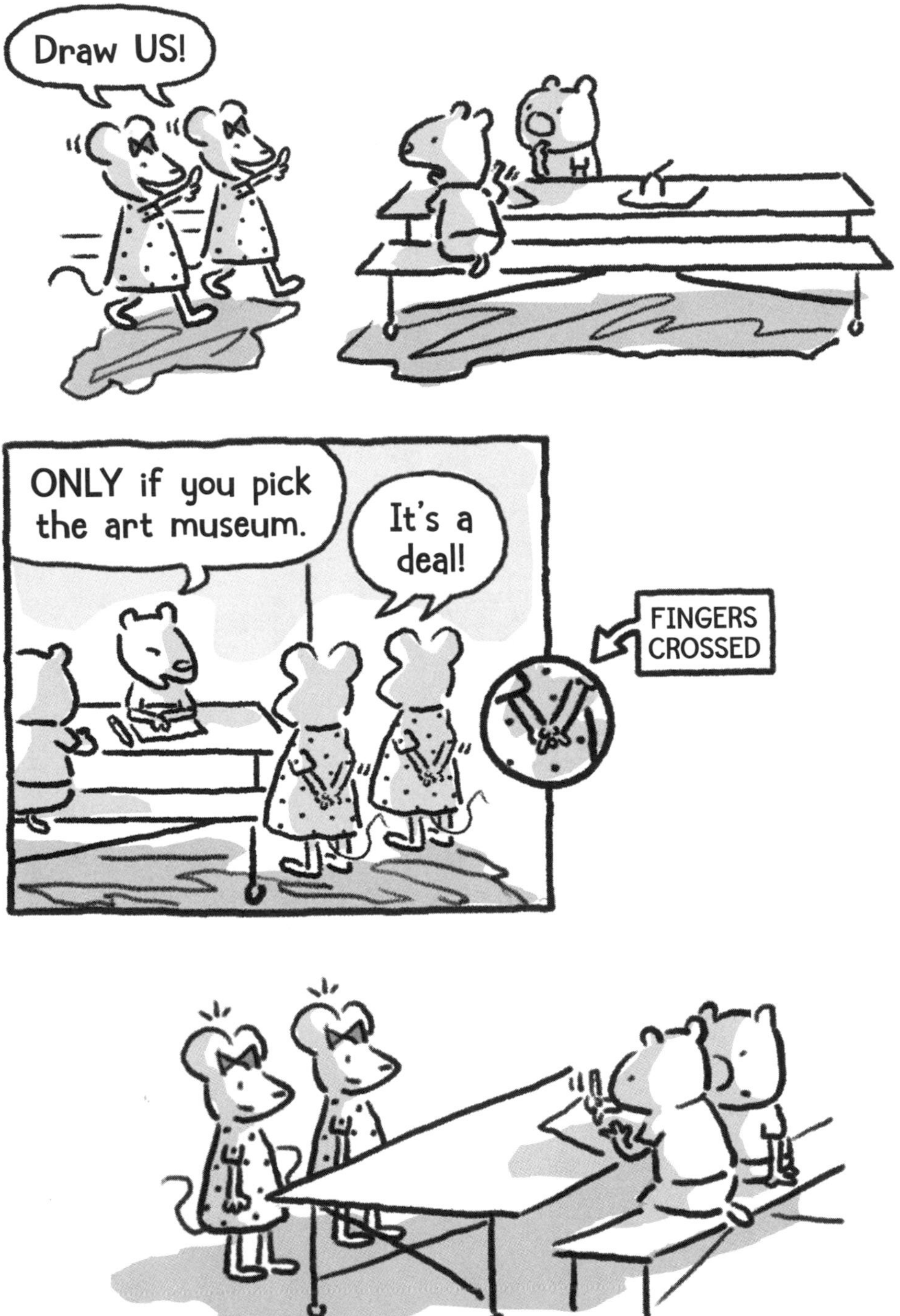
Draw US!
ONLY if you pick the art museum.
It's a deal!
FINGERS CROSSED

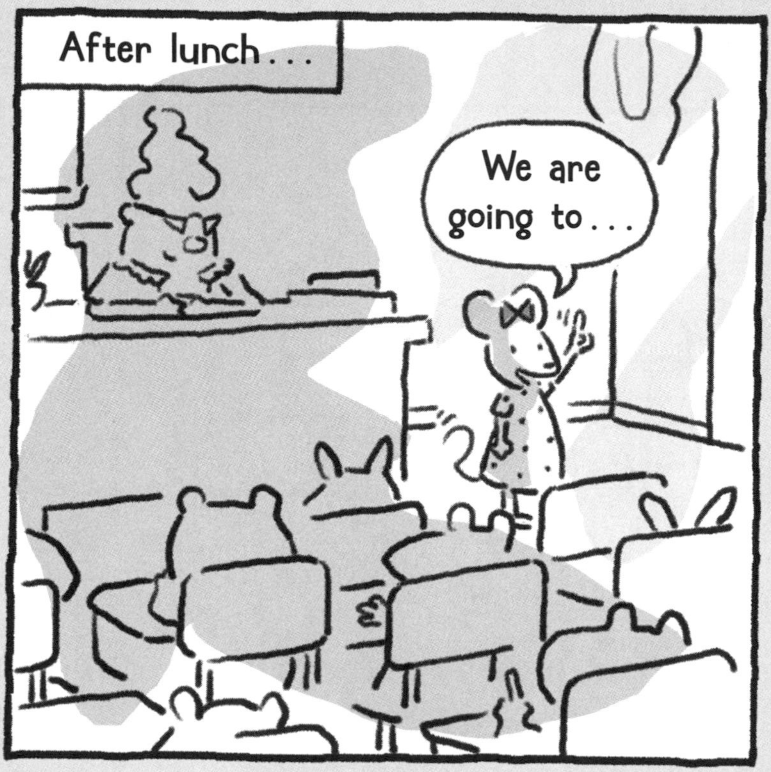
After lunch . . .
We are going to . . .

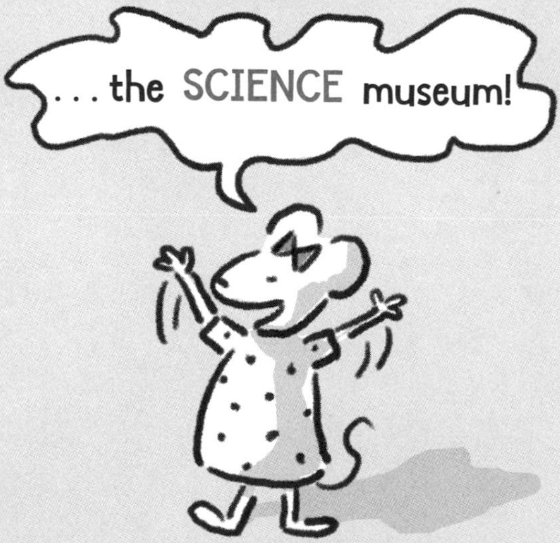
. . . the SCIENCE museum!

HANNA &
ANNA
B·A·N·A·N·A

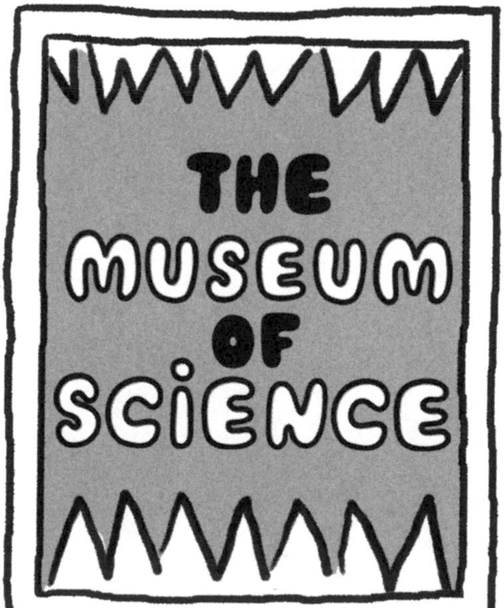
THE
MUSEUM
OF
SCIENCE

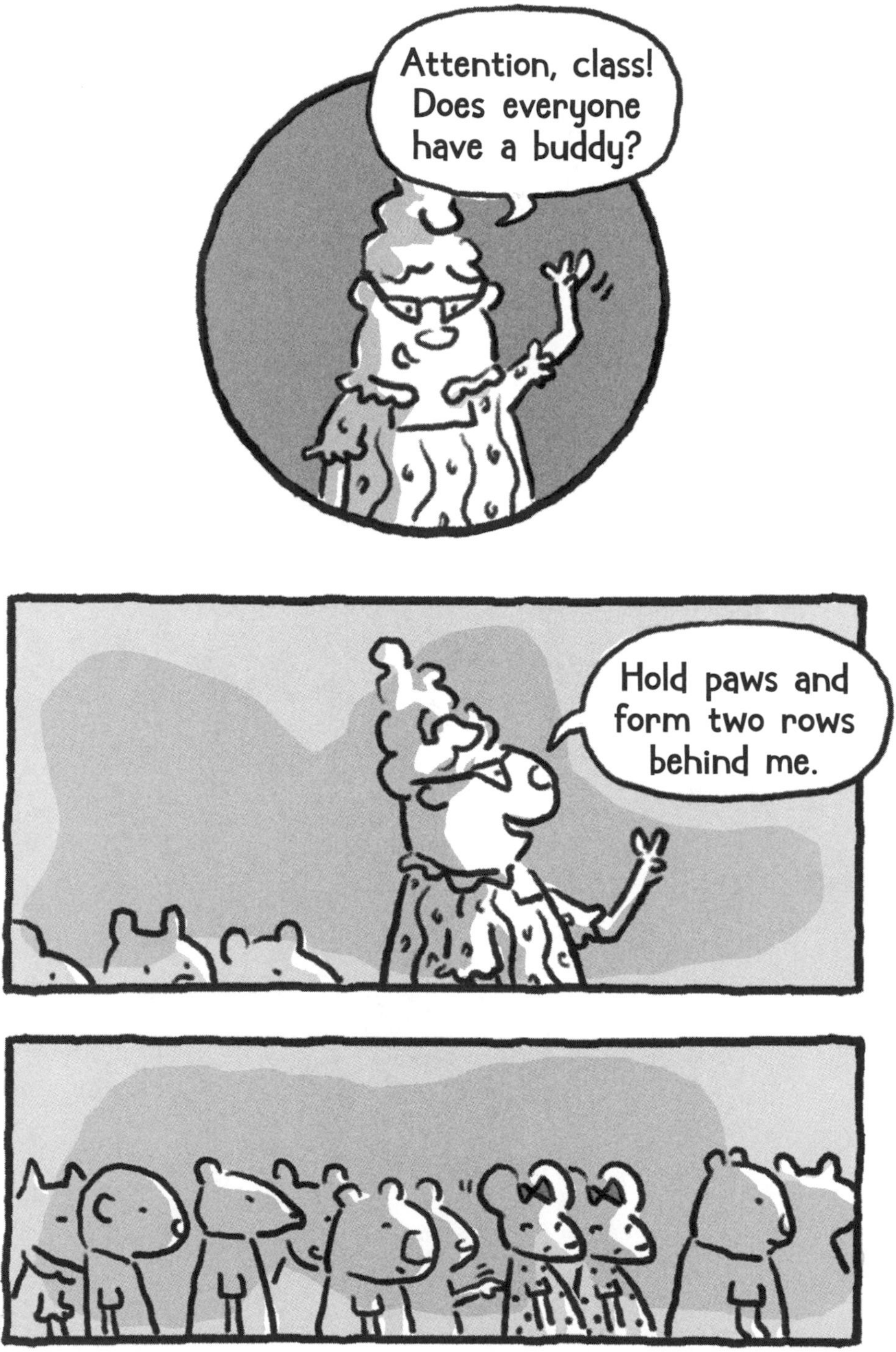
Attention, class! Does everyone have a buddy?
Hold paws and form two rows behind me.

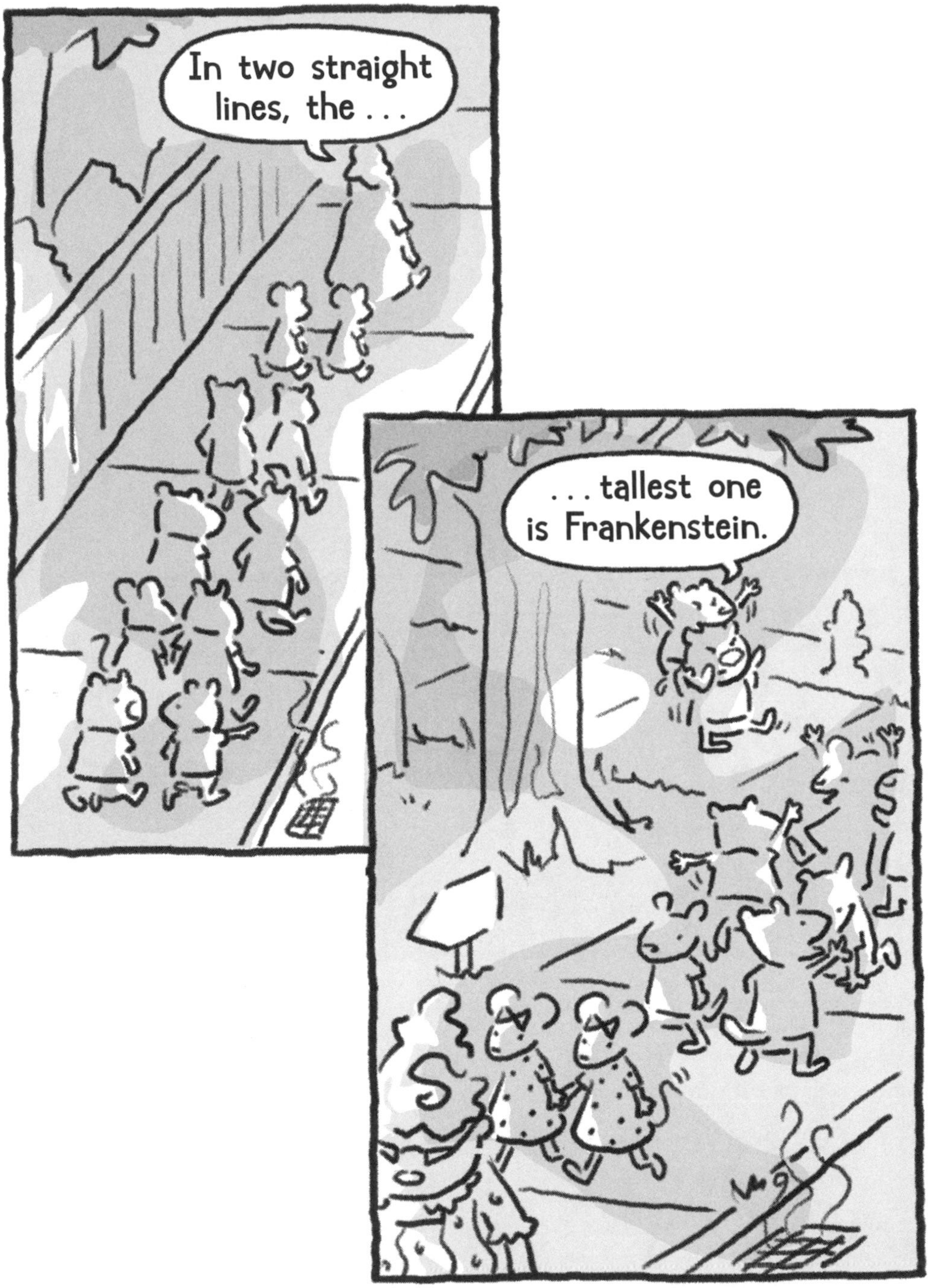
In two straight lines, the . . .
. . . tallest one is Frankenstein.

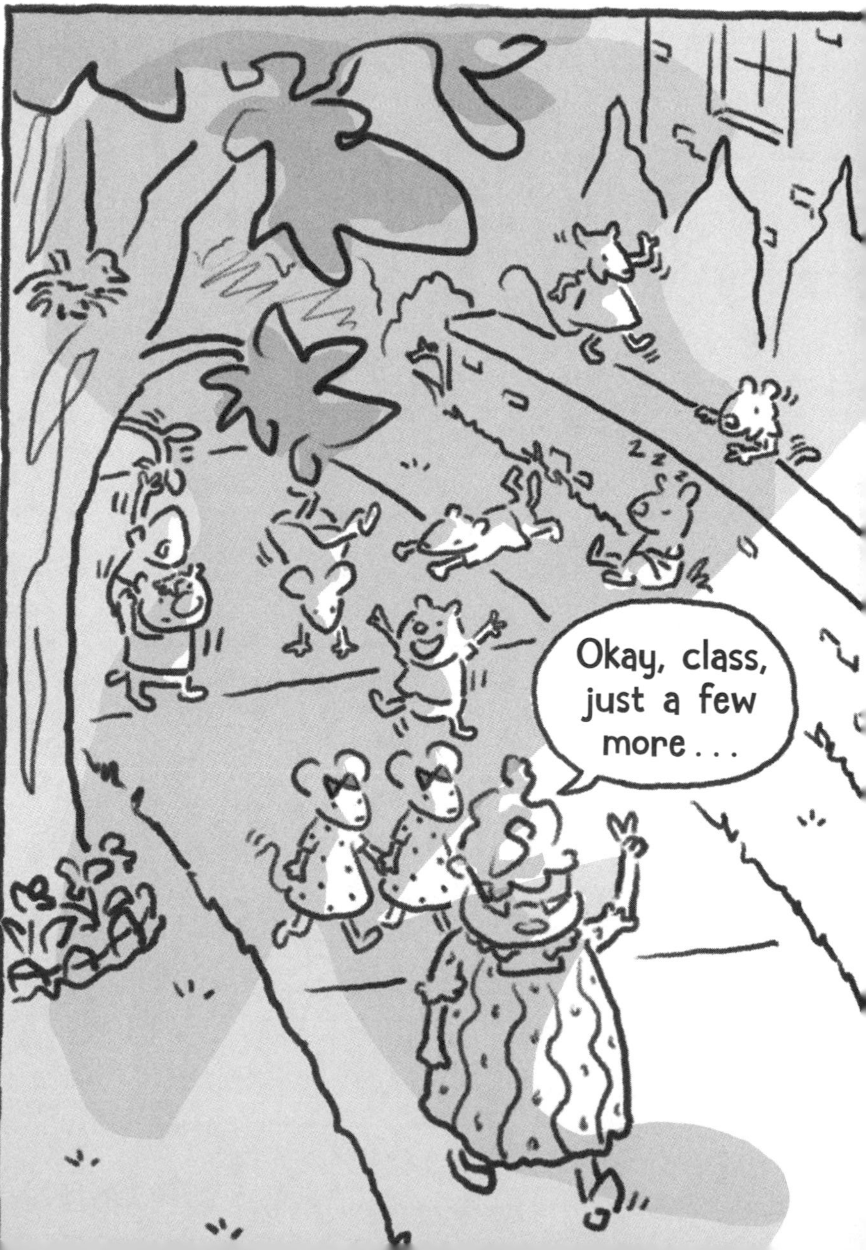
Okay, class, just a few more . . .

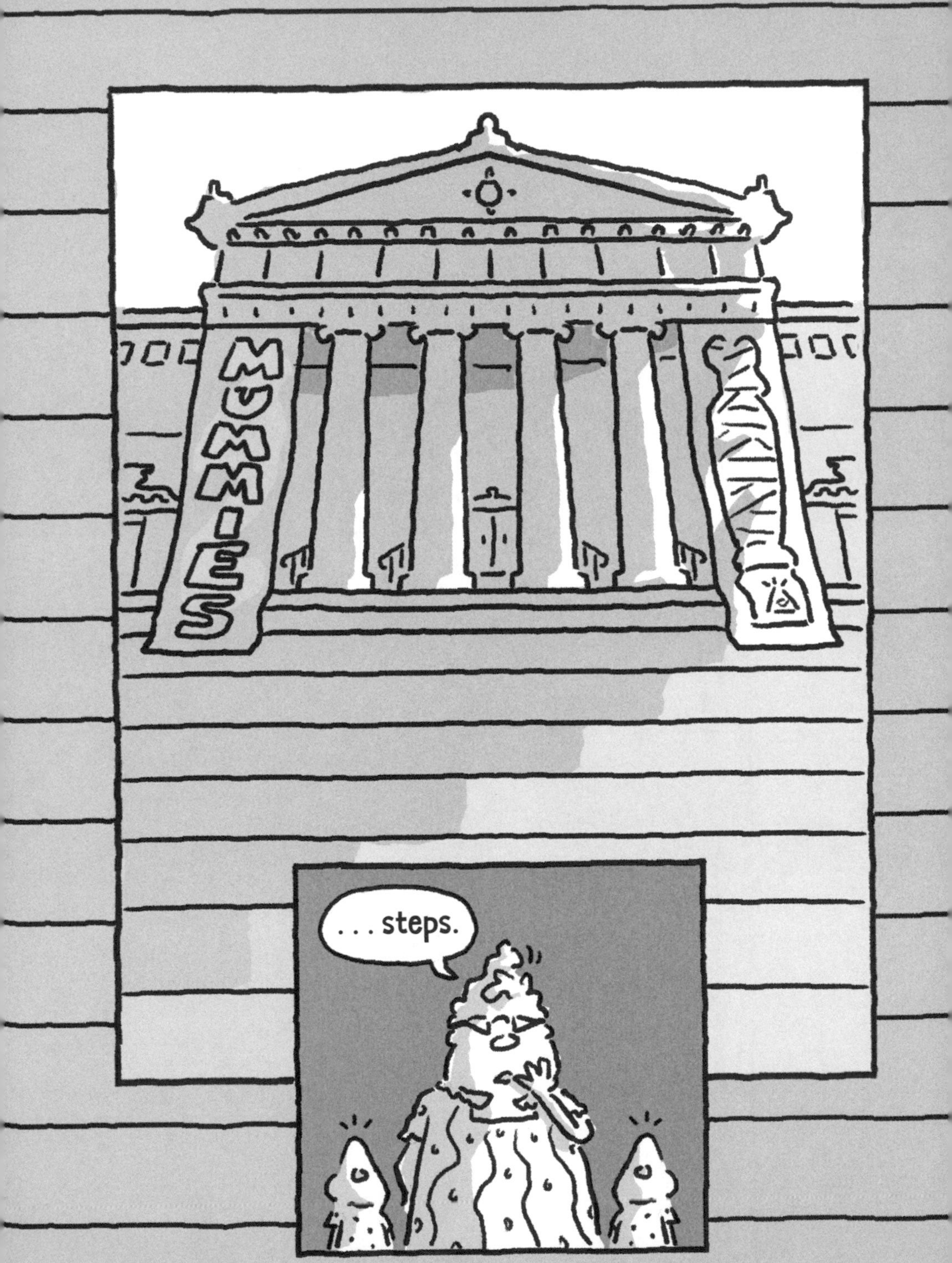
MUMMIES
. . . steps.

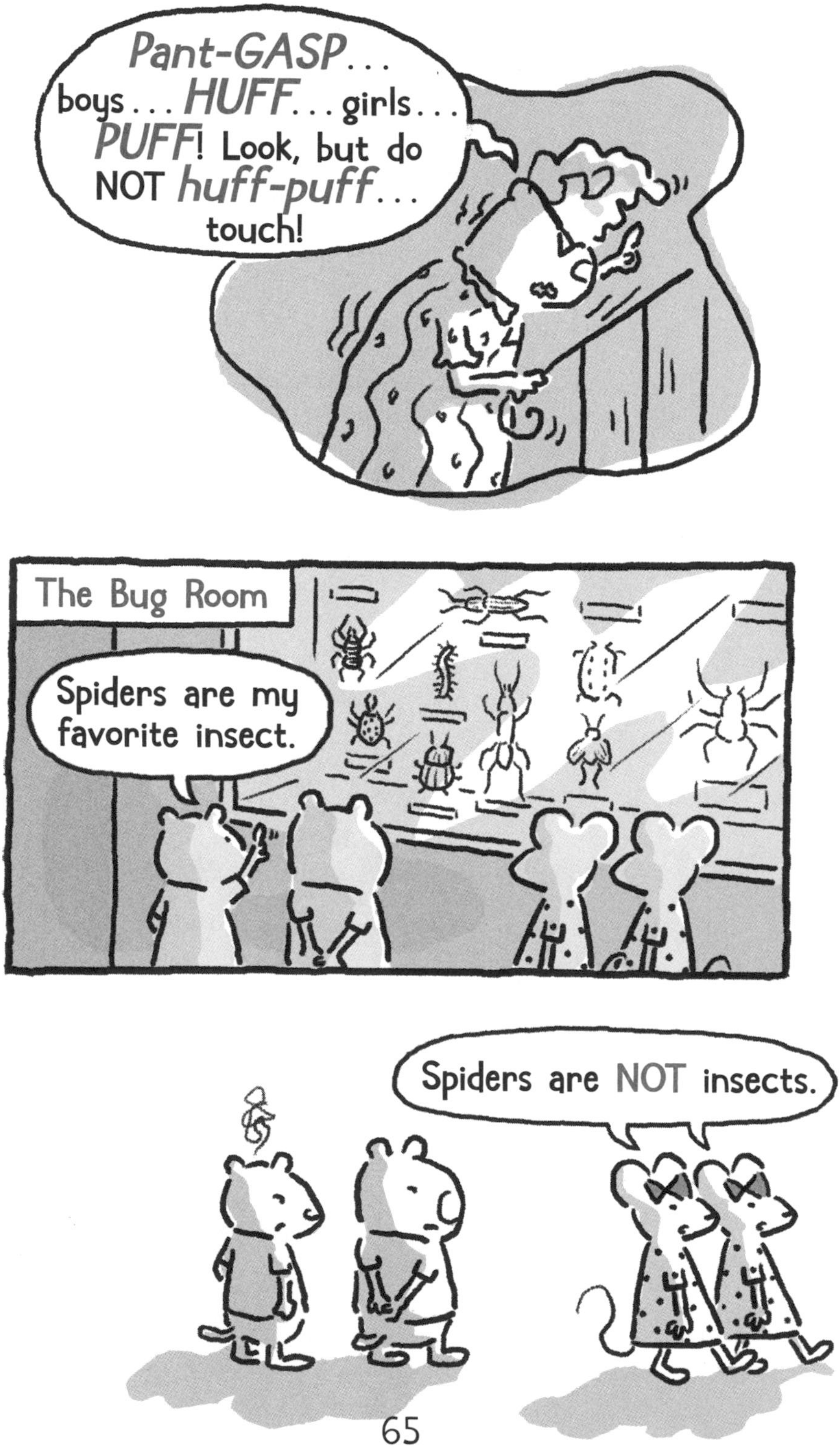
Pant-GASP... boys... HUFF... girls... PUFF! Look, but do NOT huff-puff... touch!
The Bug Room
Spiders are my favorite insect.
Spiders are NOT insects.

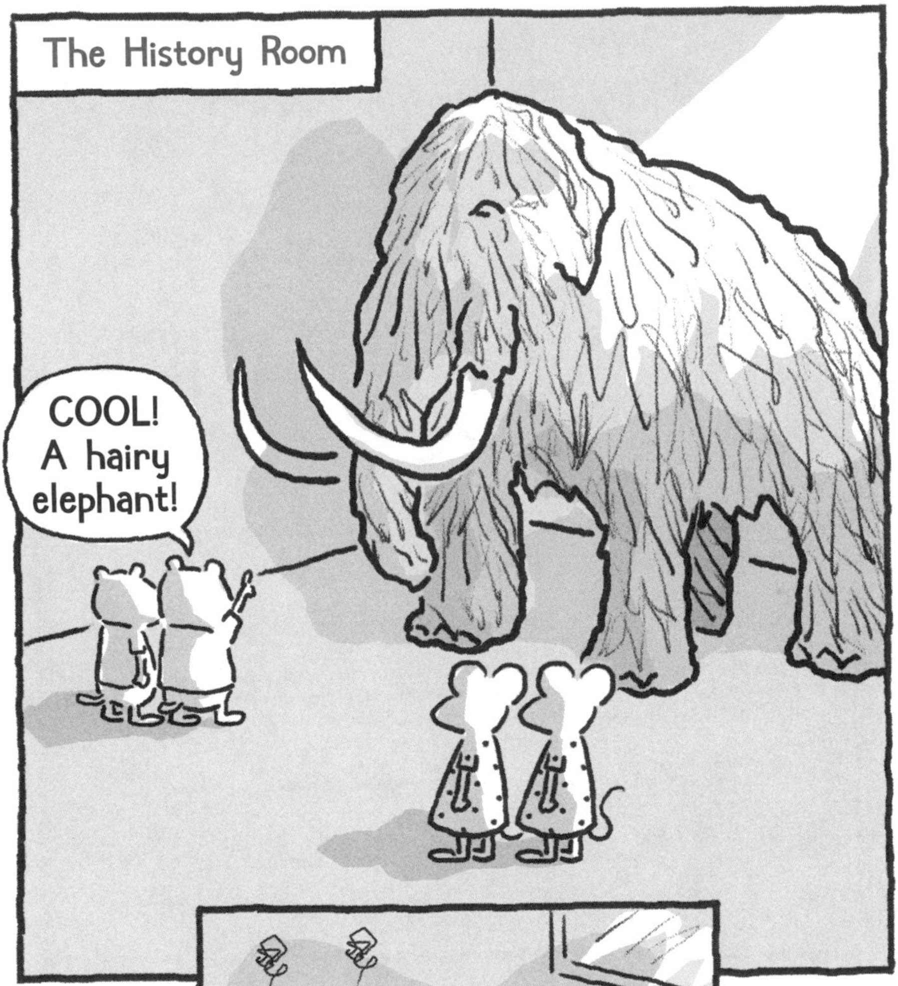
The History Room
COOL! A hairy elephant!

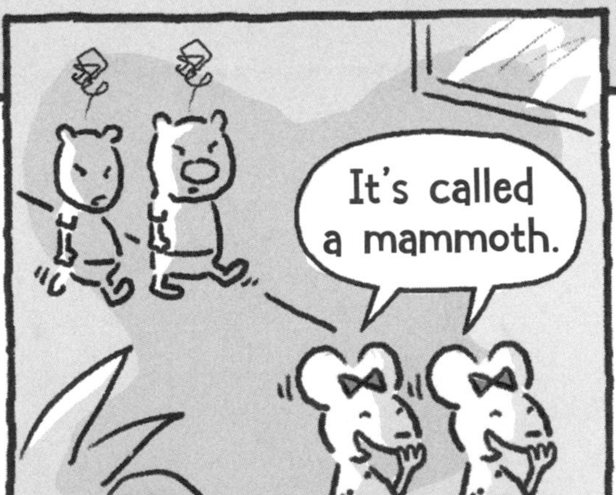
It's called a mammoth.

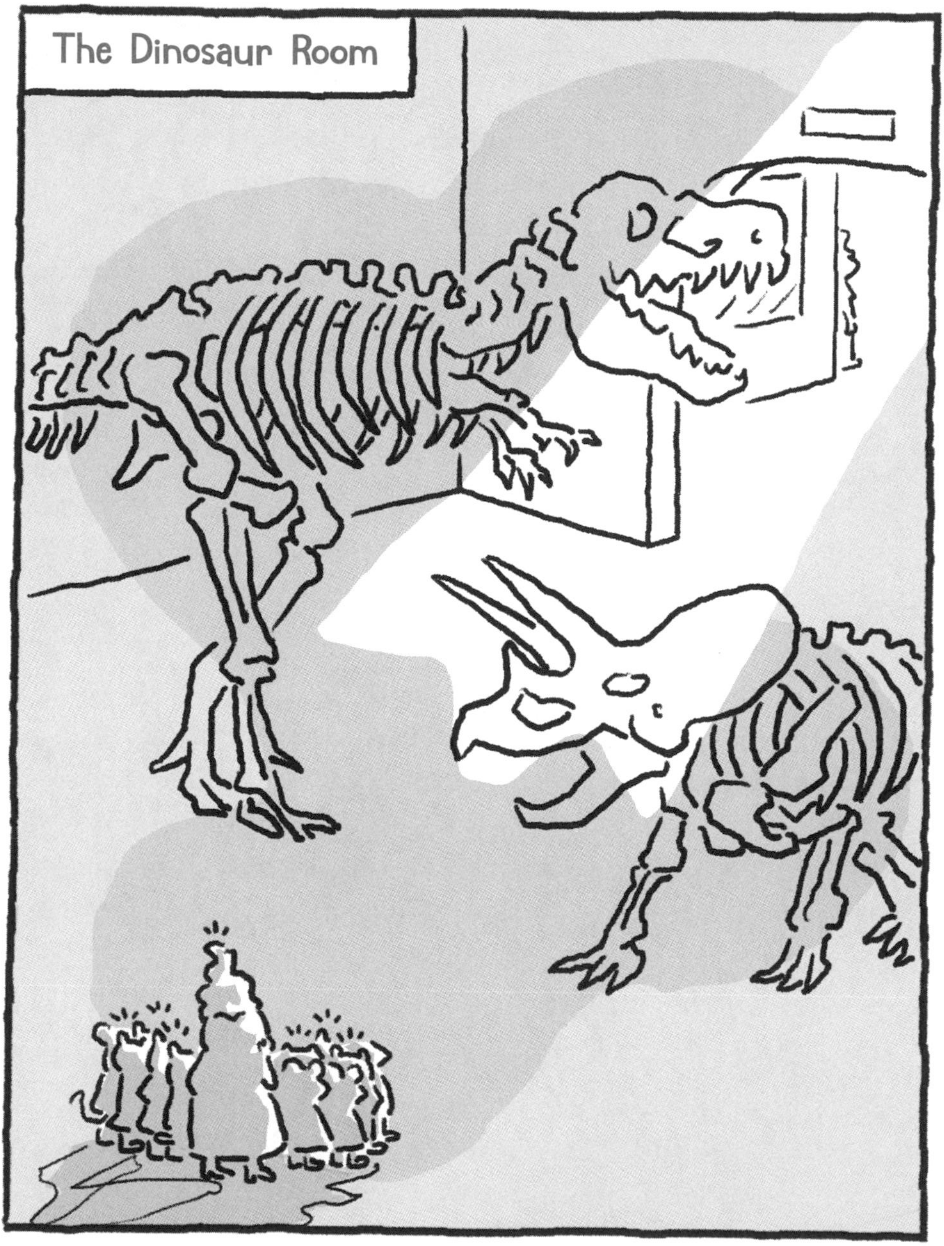
The Dinosaur Room

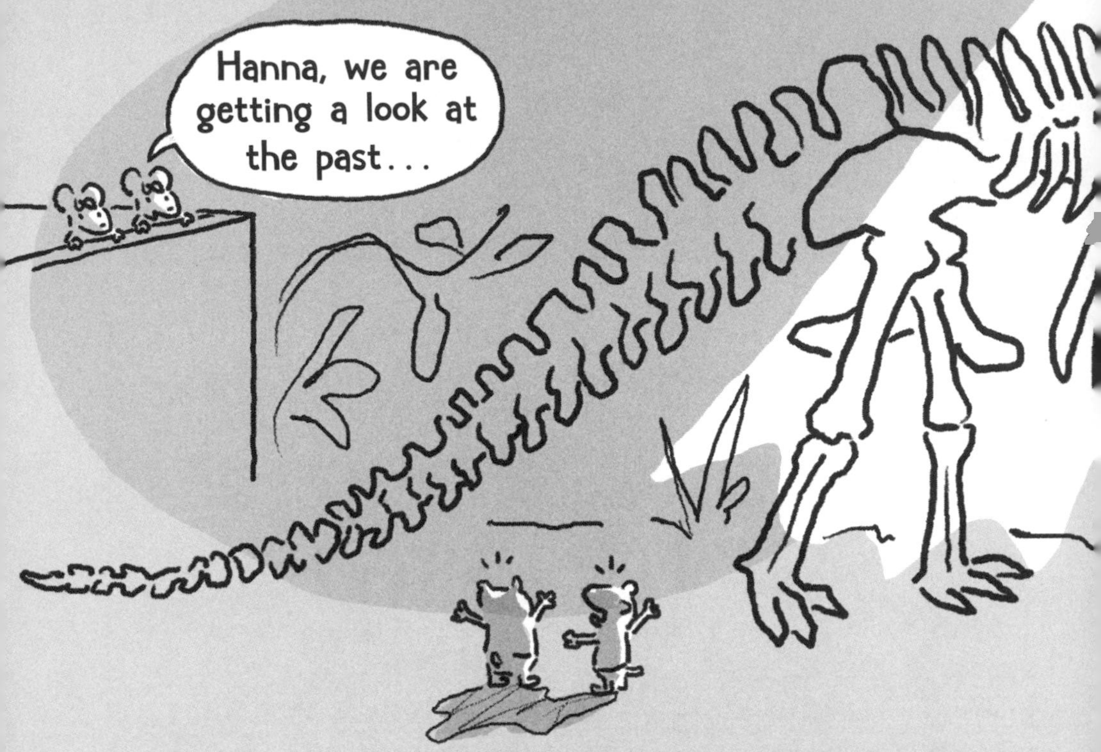
Hanna, we are getting a look at the past...

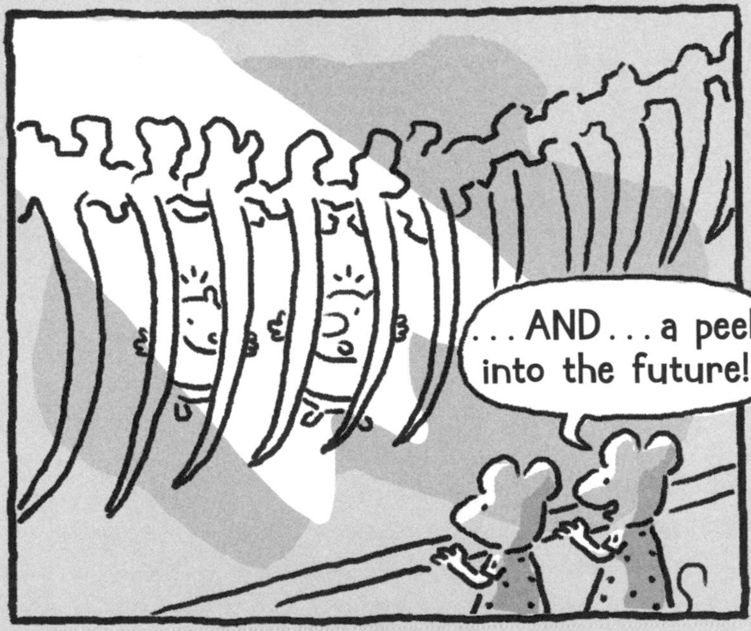
...AND...a peek into the future!

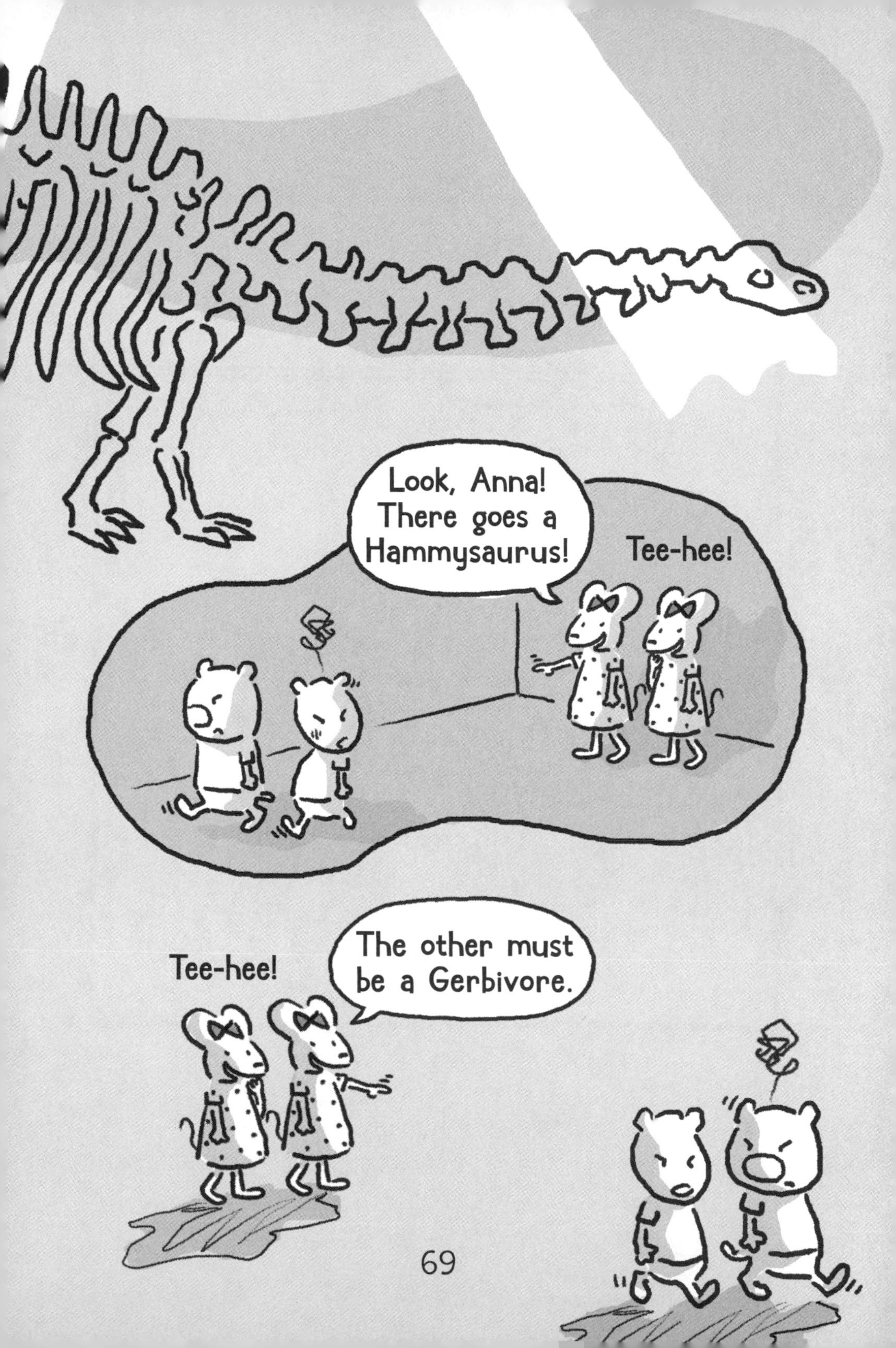
Look, Anna! There goes a Hammysaurus!
Tee-hee!
Tee-hee!
The other must be a Gerbivore.

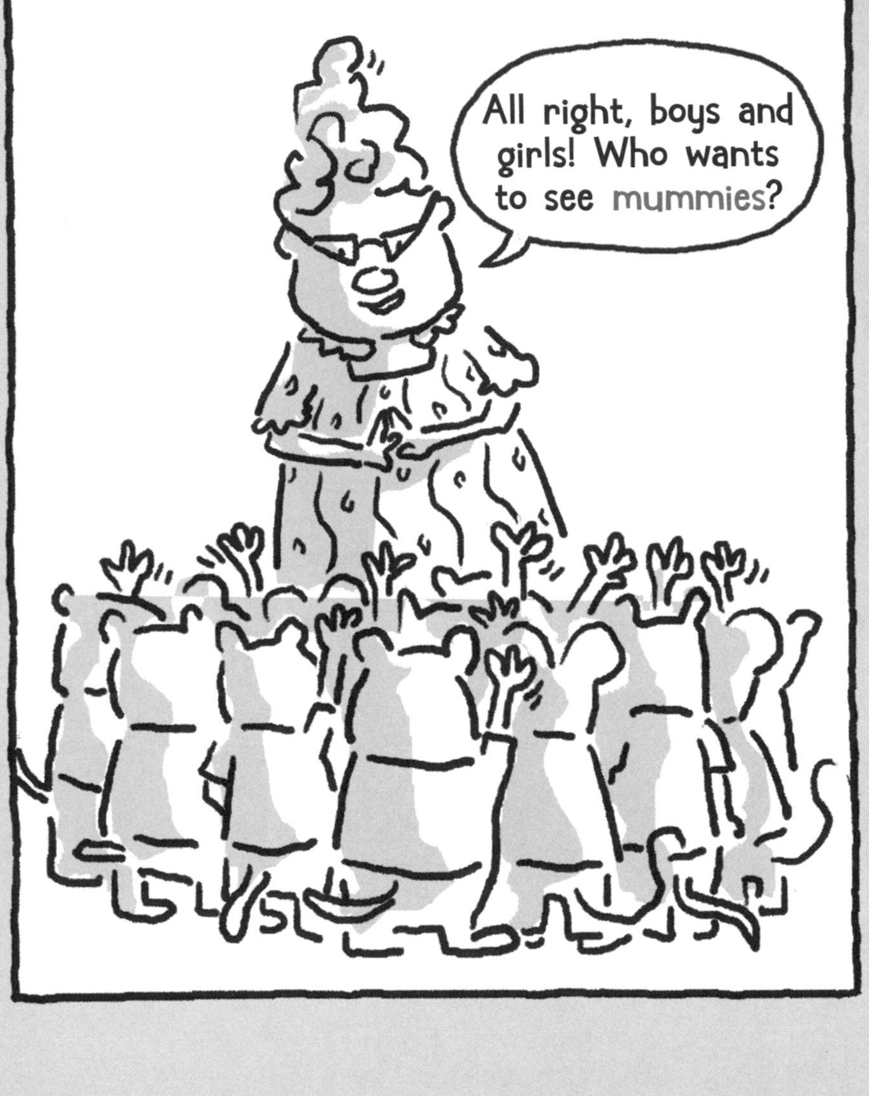
All right, boys and girls! Who wants to see mummies?

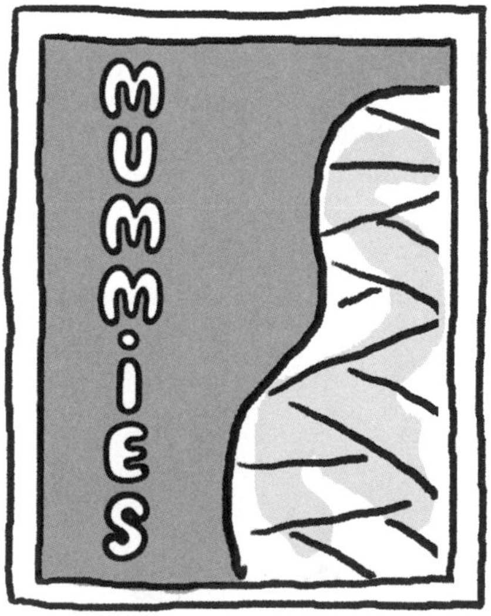
MUMMIES

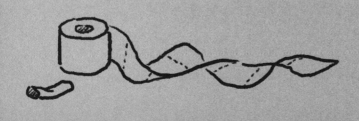

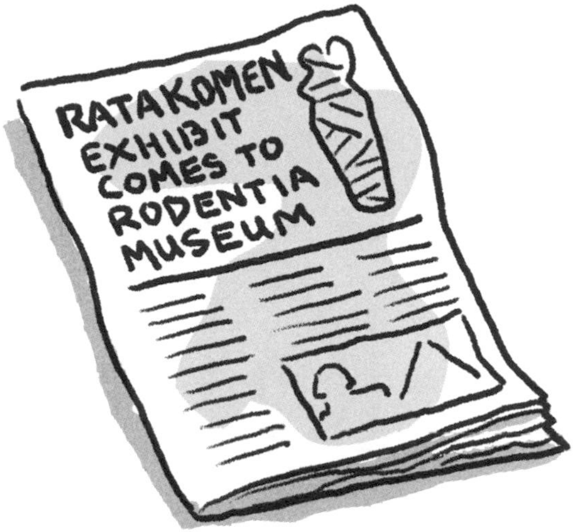
RATAKOMEN EXHIBIT COMES TO RODENTIA MUSEUM

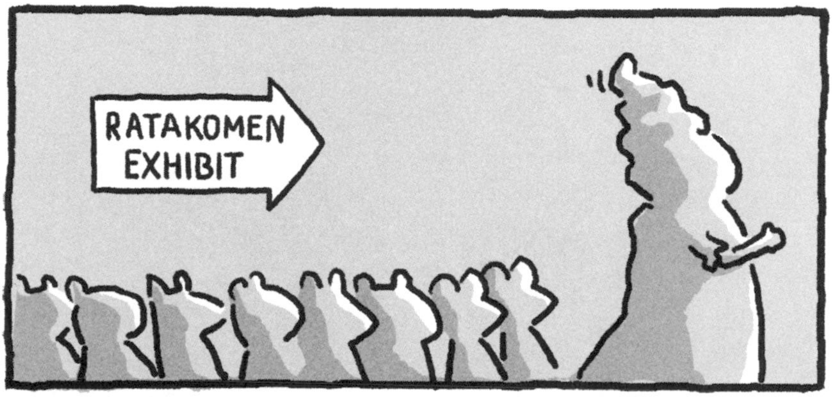
RATAKOMEN EXHIBIT

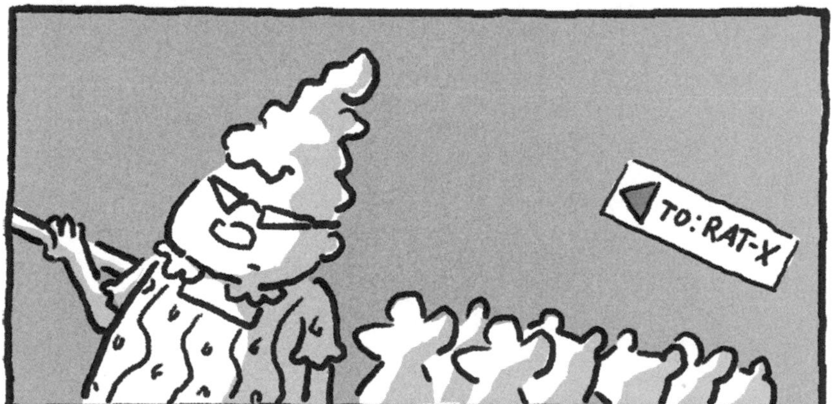
TO: RAT-X

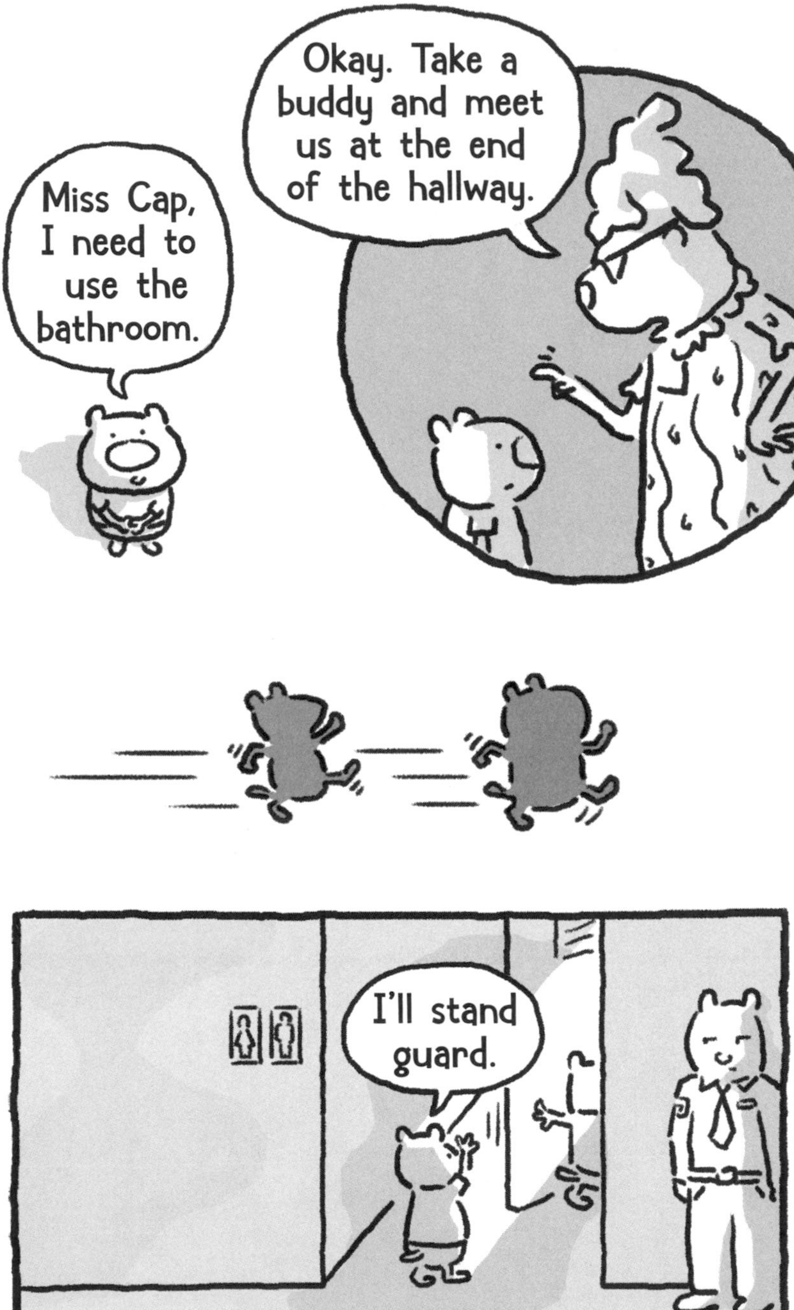
Miss Cap, I need to use the bathroom.
Okay. Take a buddy and meet us at the end of the hallway.
I'll stand guard.

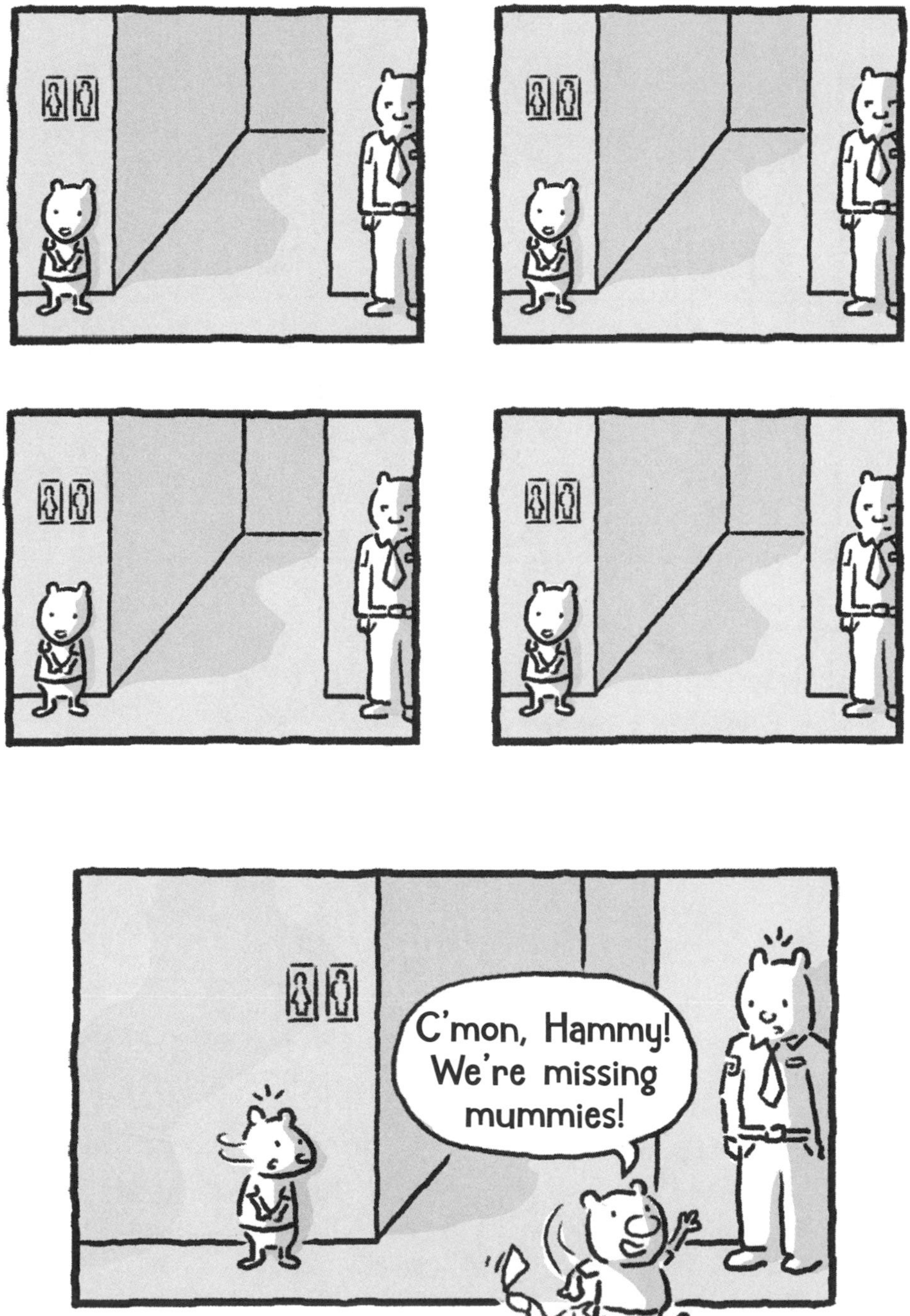
C'mon, Hammy! We're missing mummies!

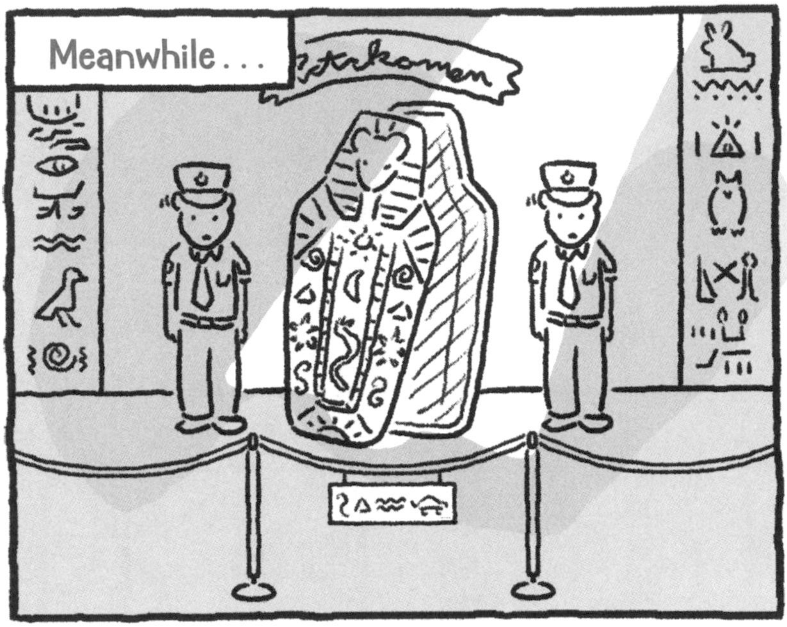
Meanwhile . . .

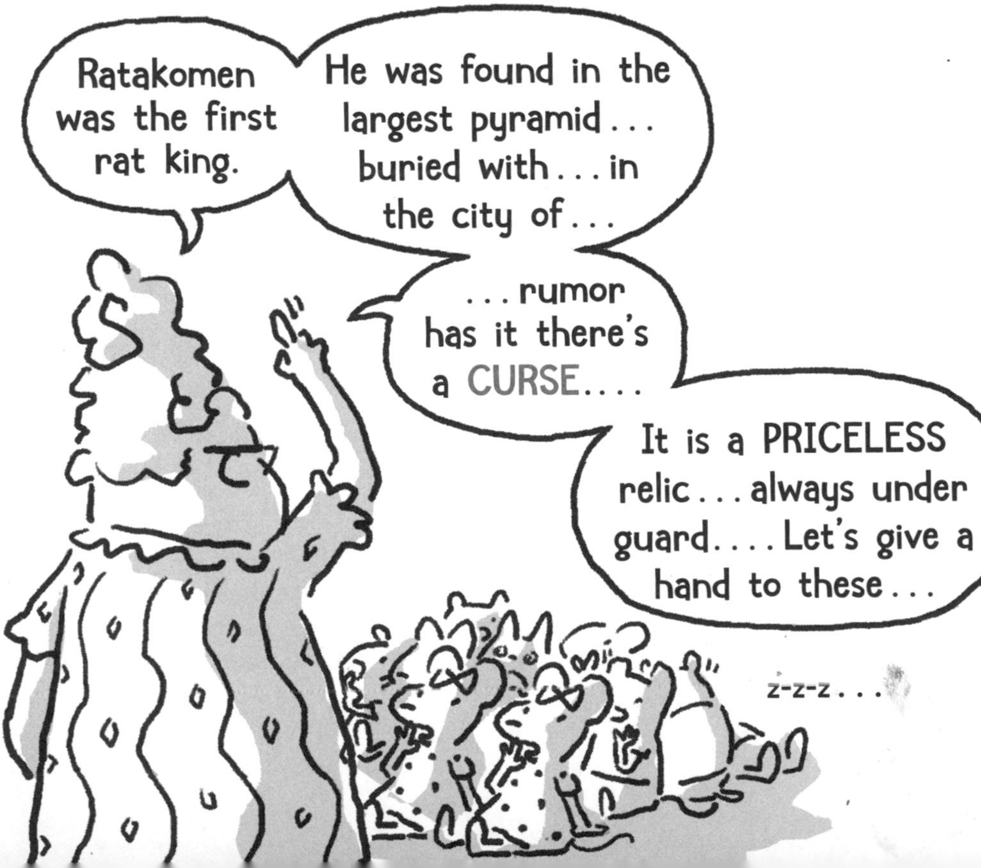
Ratakomen was the first rat king.
He was found in the largest pyramid . . . buried with . . . in the city of . . .
. . . rumor has it there's a CURSE. . . .
It is a PRICELESS relic . . . always under guard. . . . Let's give a hand to these . . .
z-z-z . . .

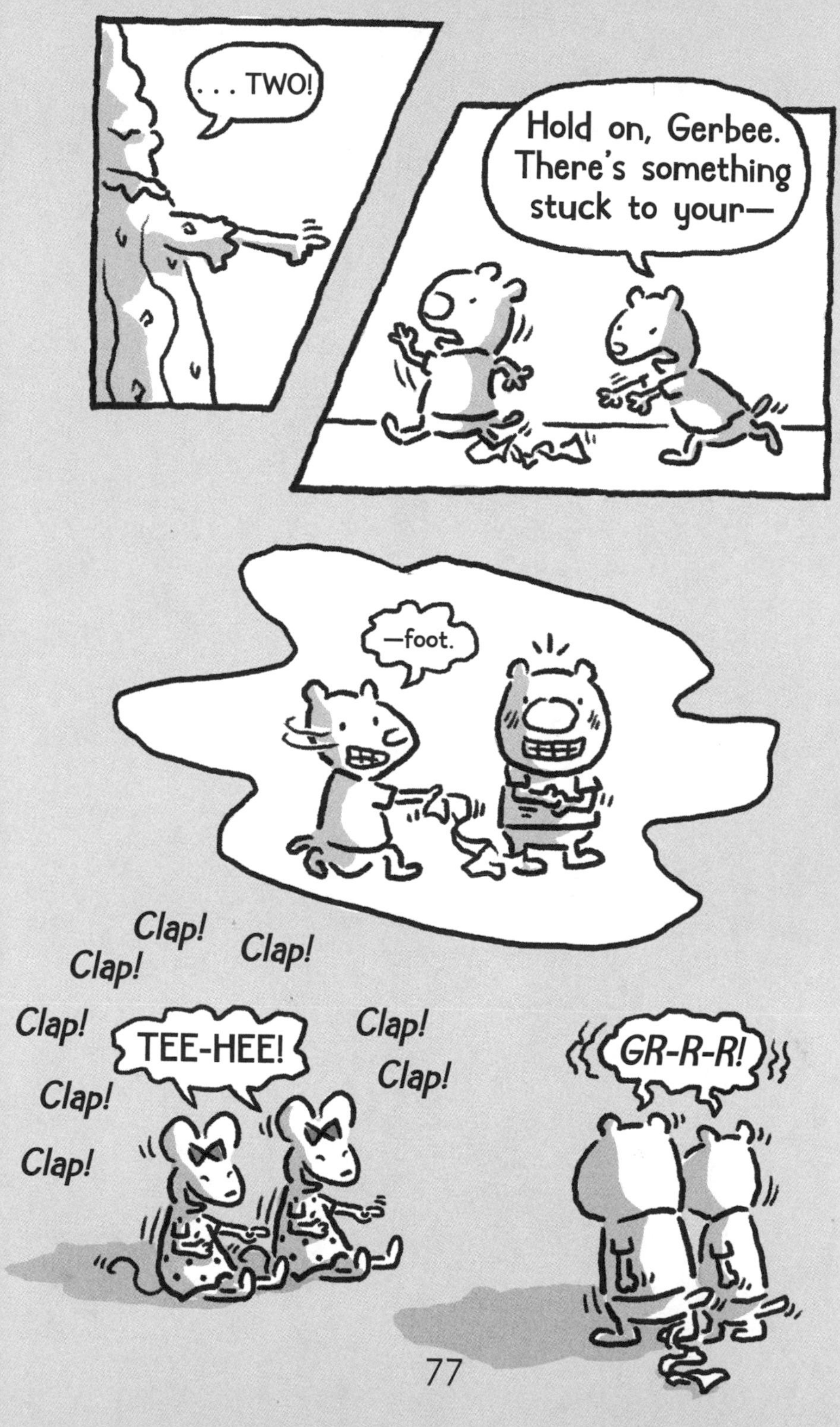
. . . TWO!
Hold on, Gerbee. There's something stuck to your—
—foot.
Clap!
Clap!
Clap!
Clap!
TEE-HEE!
Clap!
Clap!
Clap!
Clap!
GR-R-R!

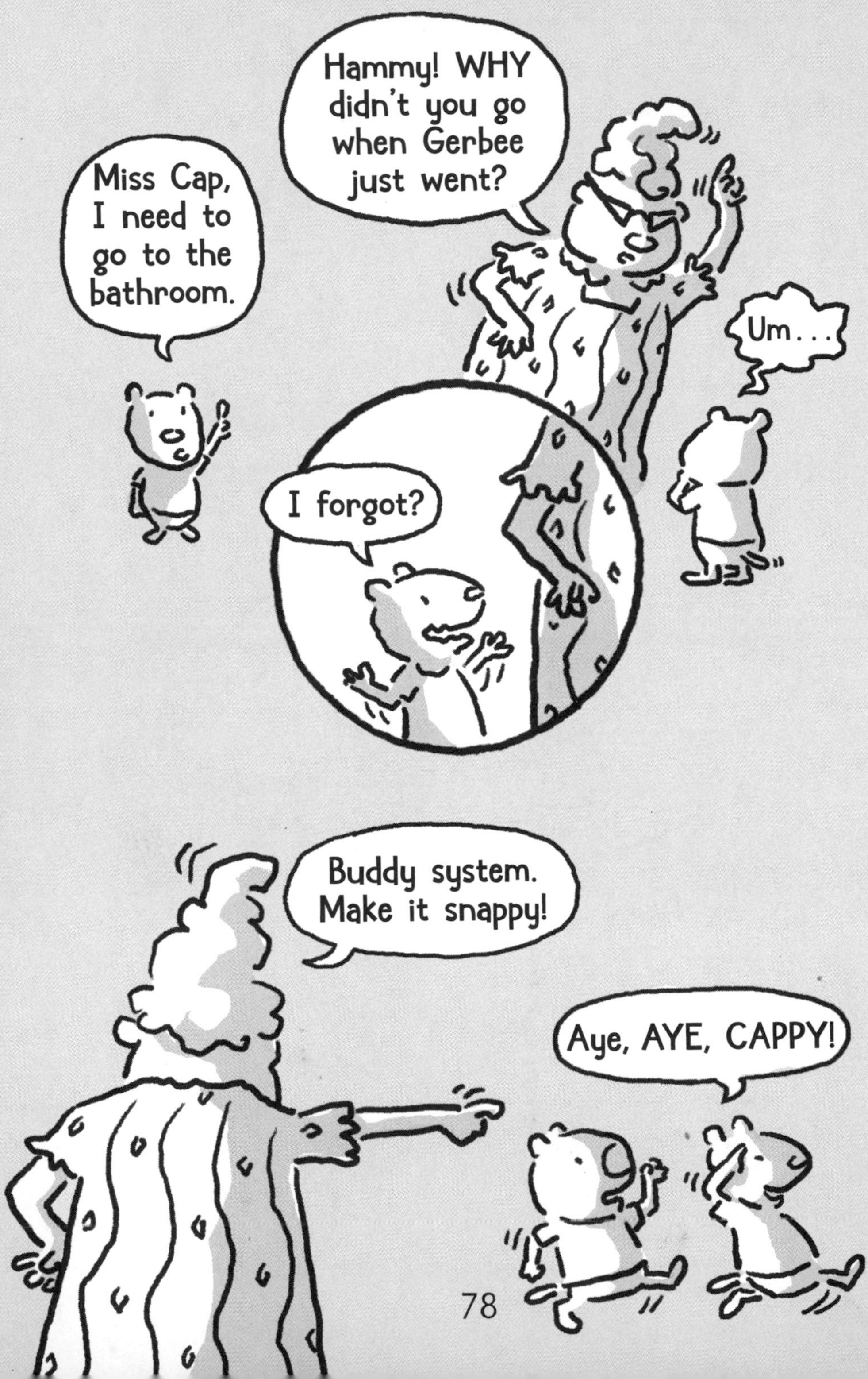
Miss Cap, I need to go to the bathroom.
Hammy! WHY didn't you go when Gerbee just went?
Um...
I forgot?
Buddy system. Make it snappy!
Aye, AYE, CAPPY!

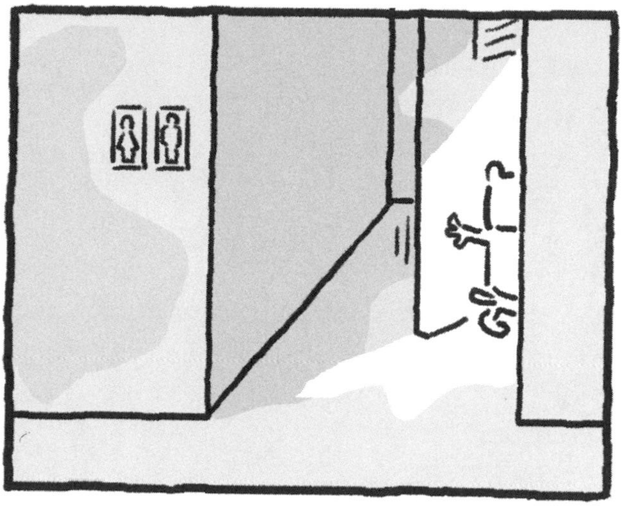

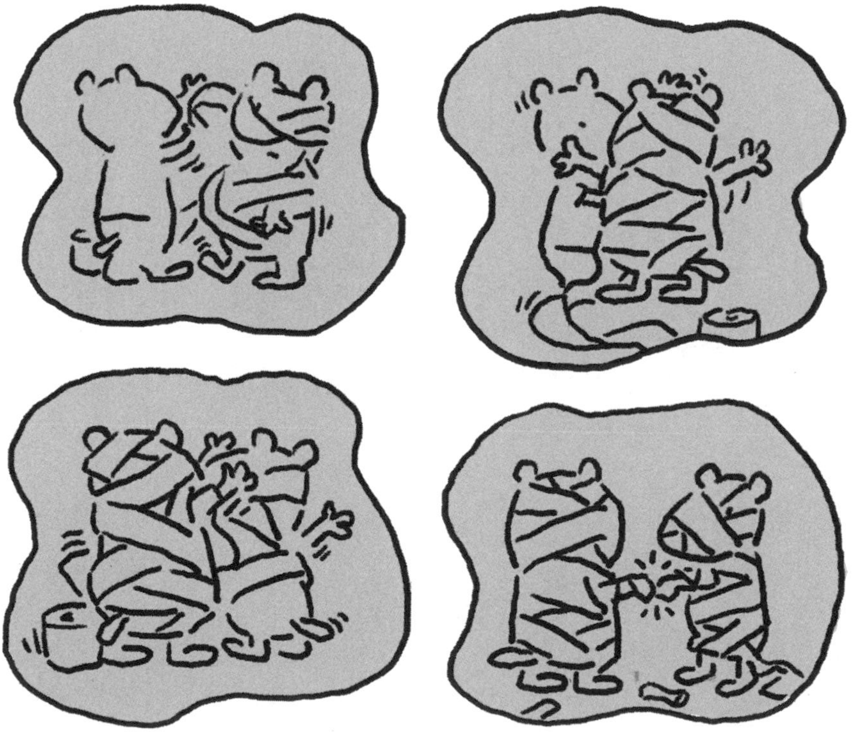

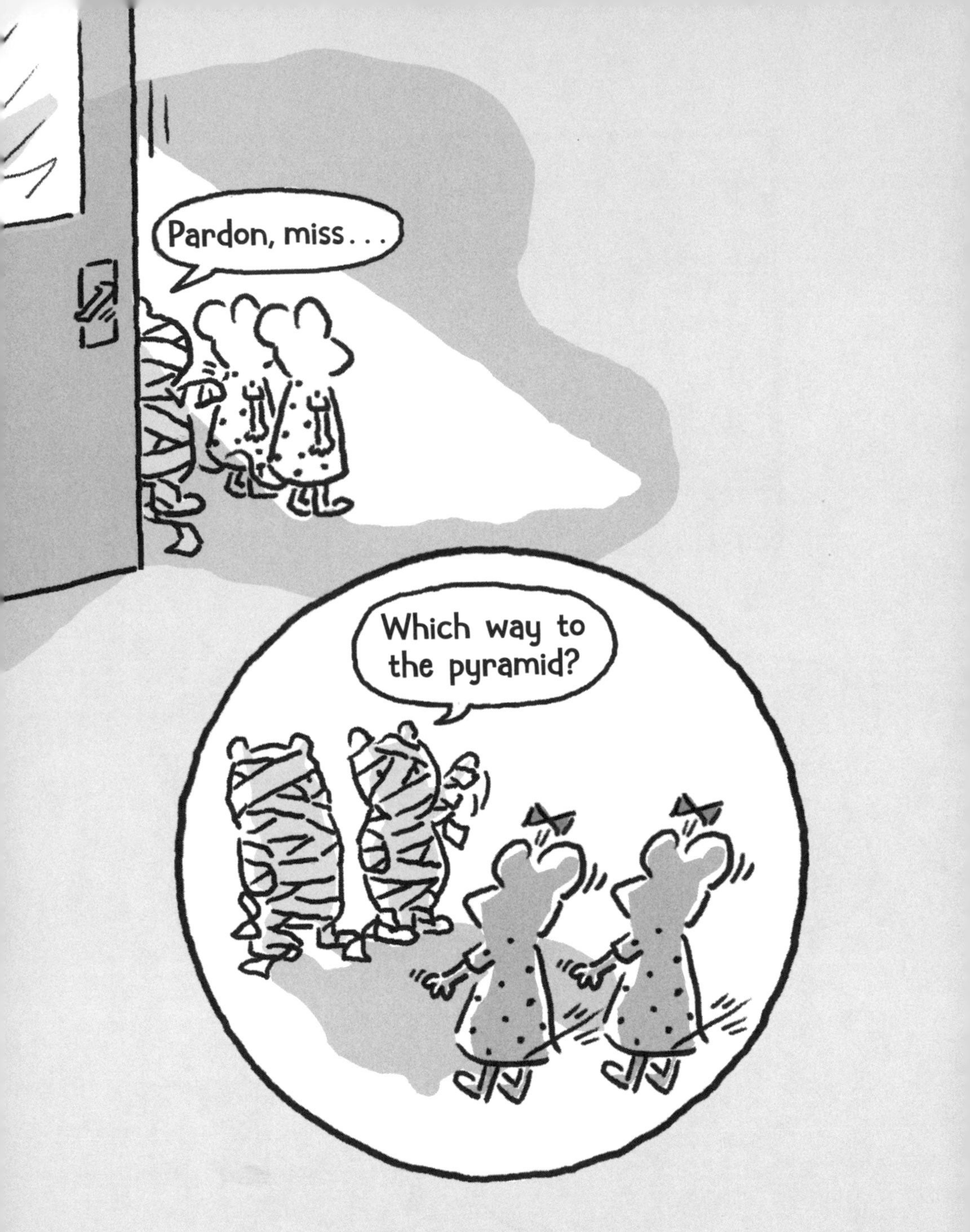
Pardon, miss. . .
Which way to the pyramid?

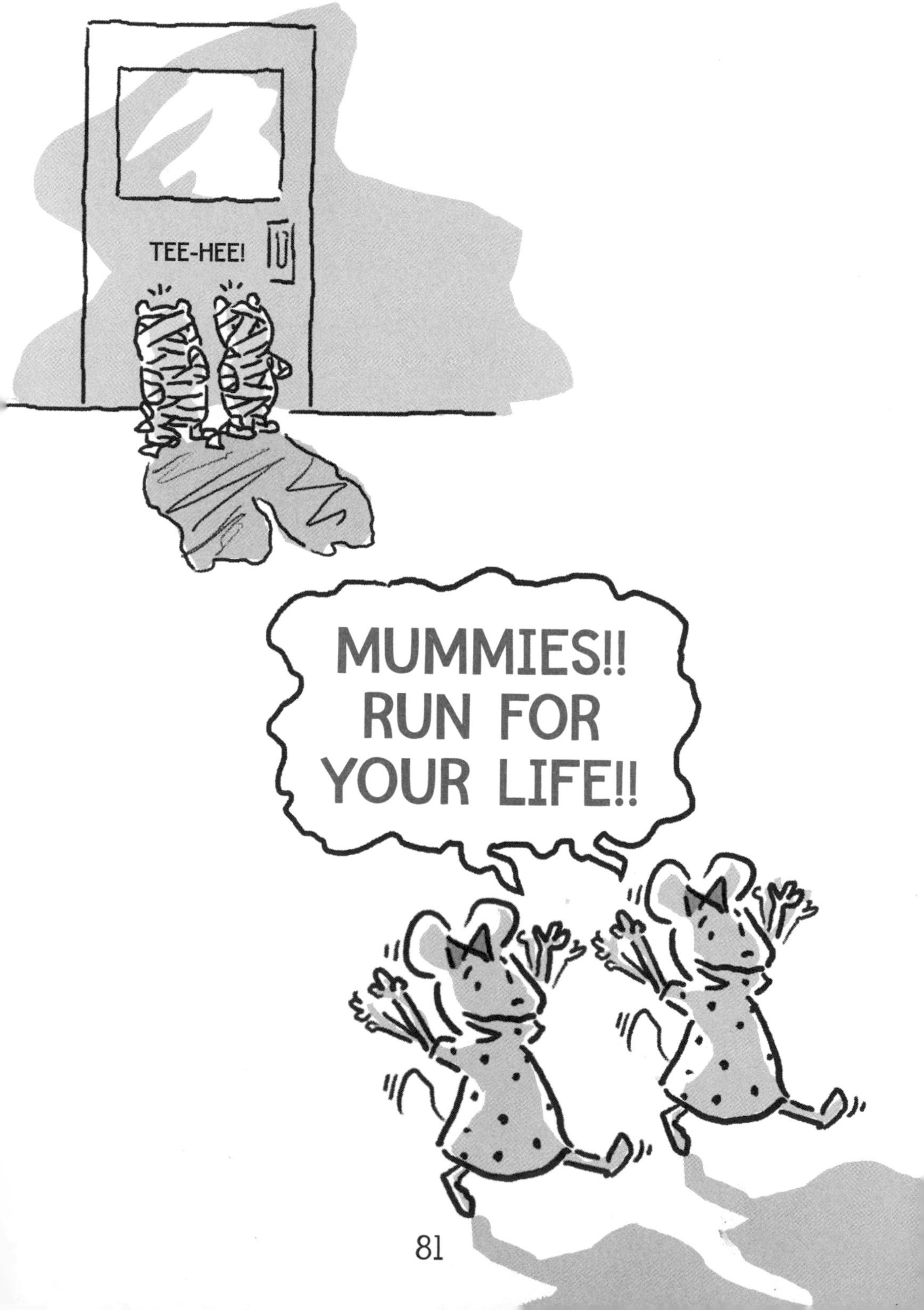
TEE-HEE!
MUMMIES!! RUN FOR YOUR LIFE!!

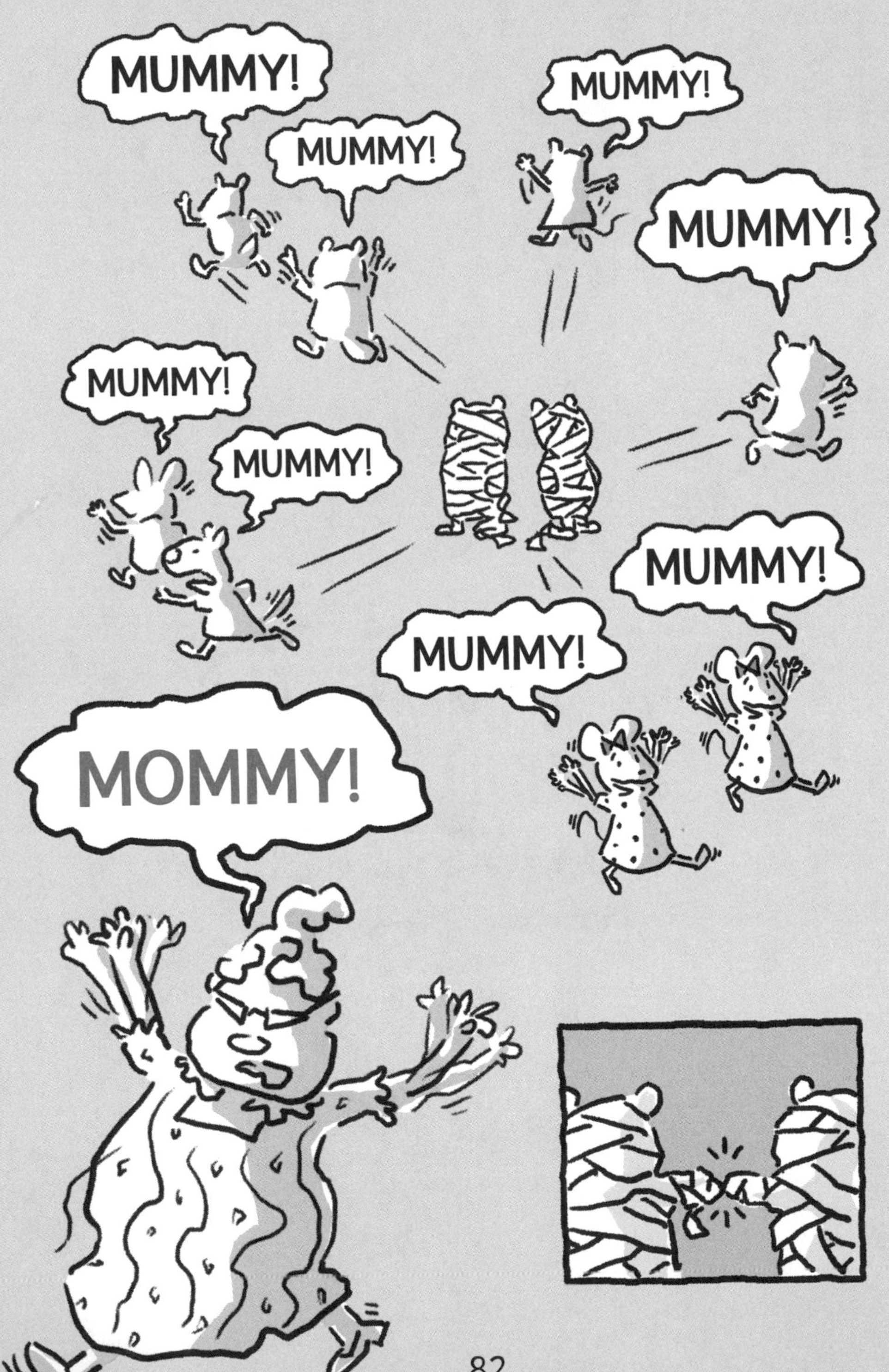
MUMMY!
MUMMY!
MUMMY!
MUMMY!
MUMMY!
MUMMY!
MUMMY!
MUMMY!
MOMMY!

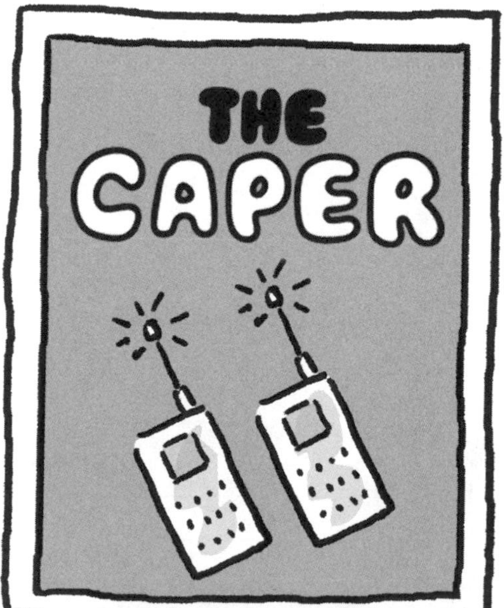
THE
CAPER

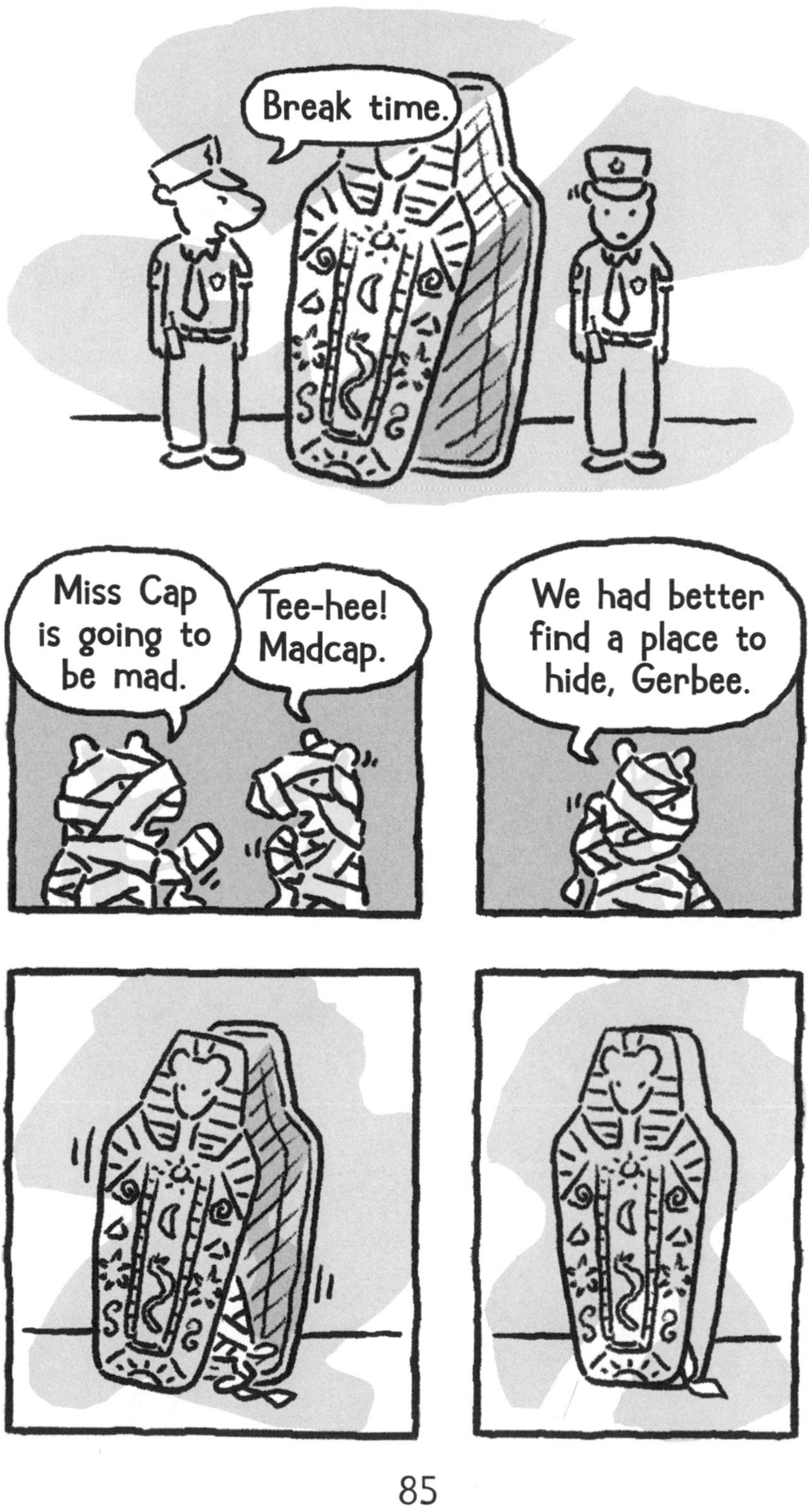
Break time.
Miss Cap is going to be mad.
Tee-hee! Madcap.
We had better find a place to hide, Gerbee.

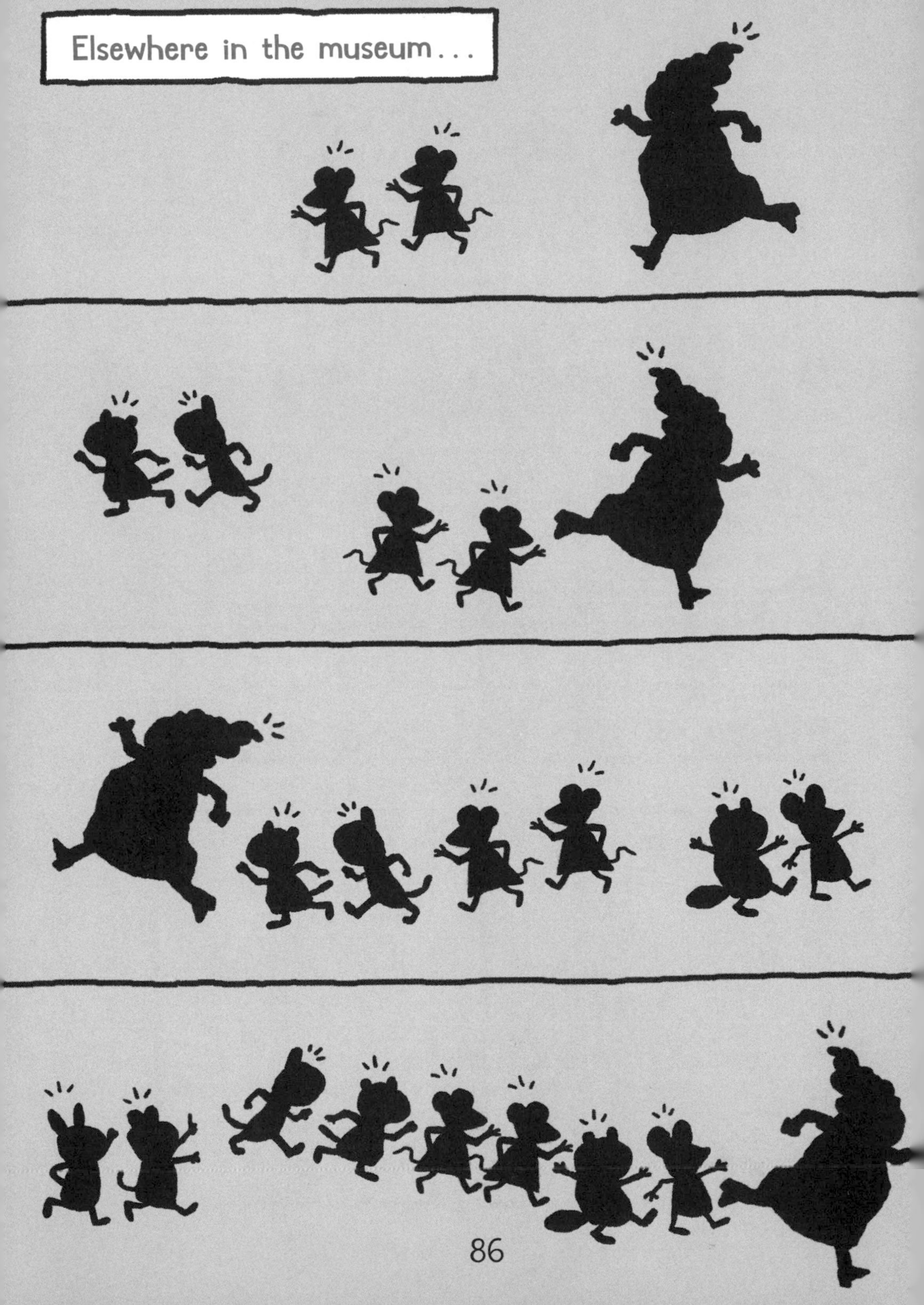
Elsewhere in the museum . . .

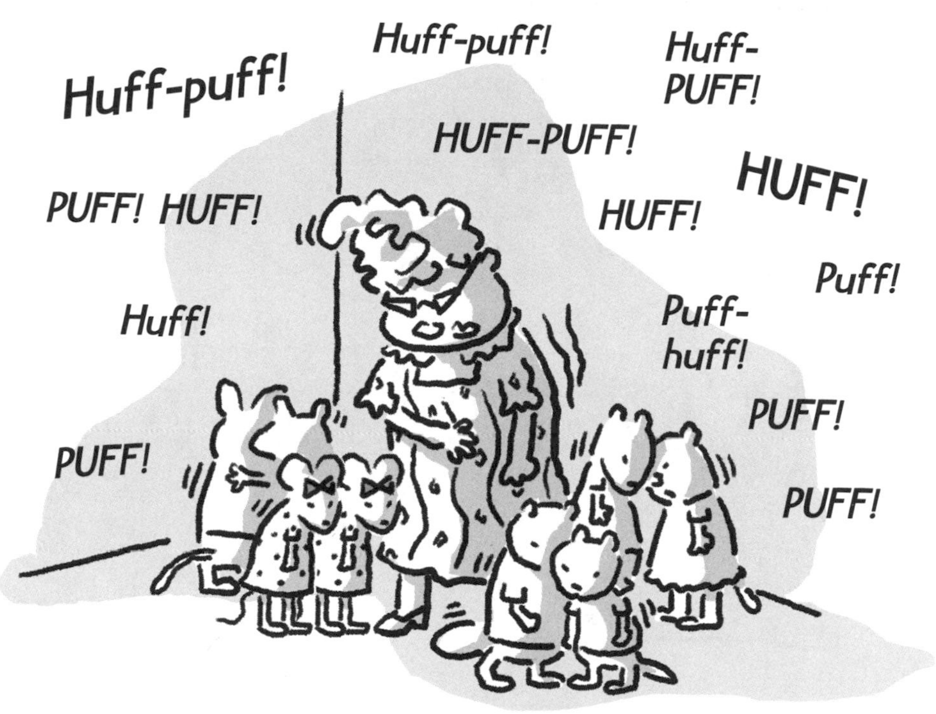
Huff-puff!
Huff-puff!
Huff-PUFF!
HUFF-PUFF!
PUFF! HUFF!
HUFF!
HUFF!
Puff!
Huff!
Puff-huff!
PUFF!
PUFF!
PUFF!

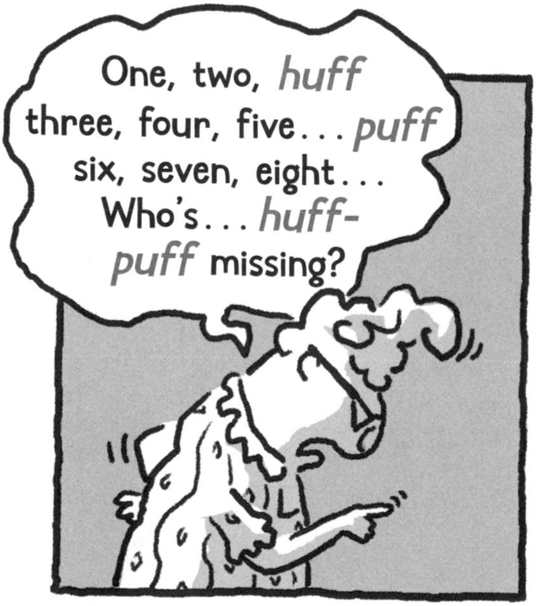
One, two, huff three, four, five... puff six, seven, eight... Who's... huff-puff missing?

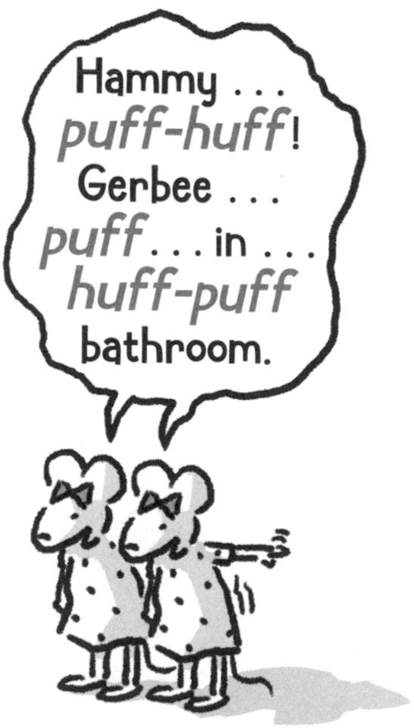
Hammy ... puff-huff! Gerbee ... puff... in ... huff-puff bathroom.

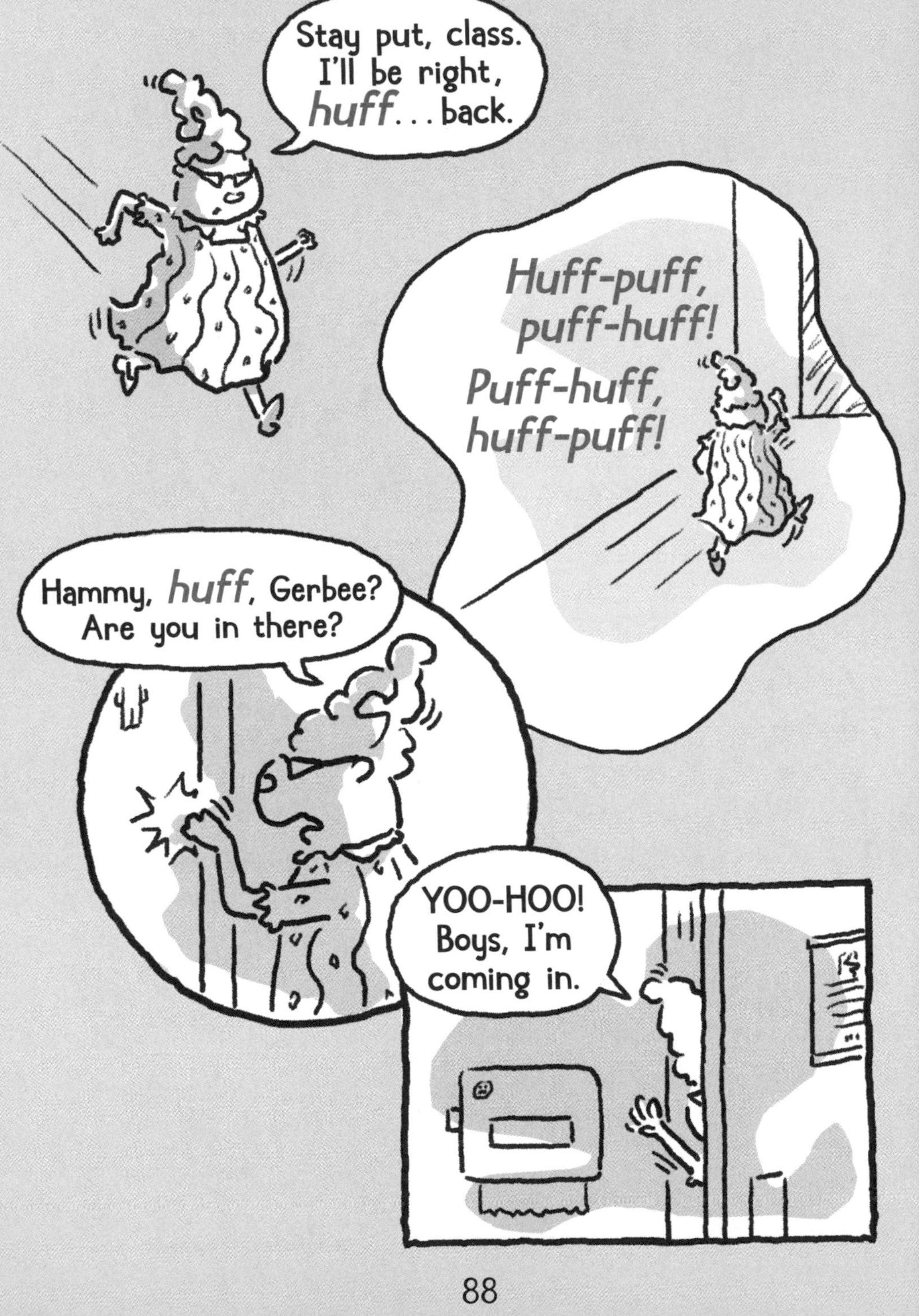
Stay put, class. I'll be right, *huff*. . . back.
Huff-puff, puff-huff!
Puff-huff, huff-puff!
Hammy, *huff*, Gerbee? Are you in there?
YOO-HOO! Boys, I'm coming in.

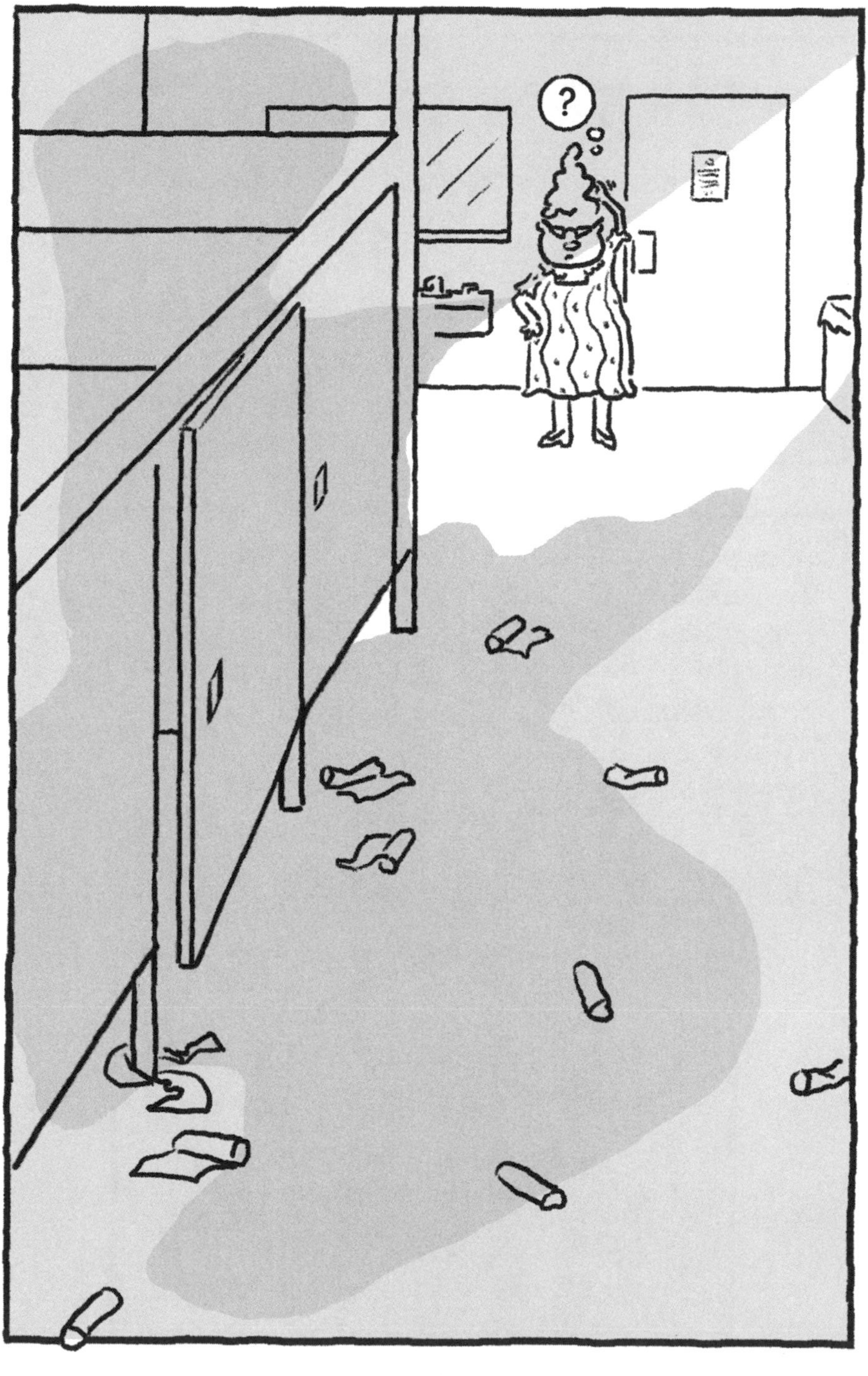
?

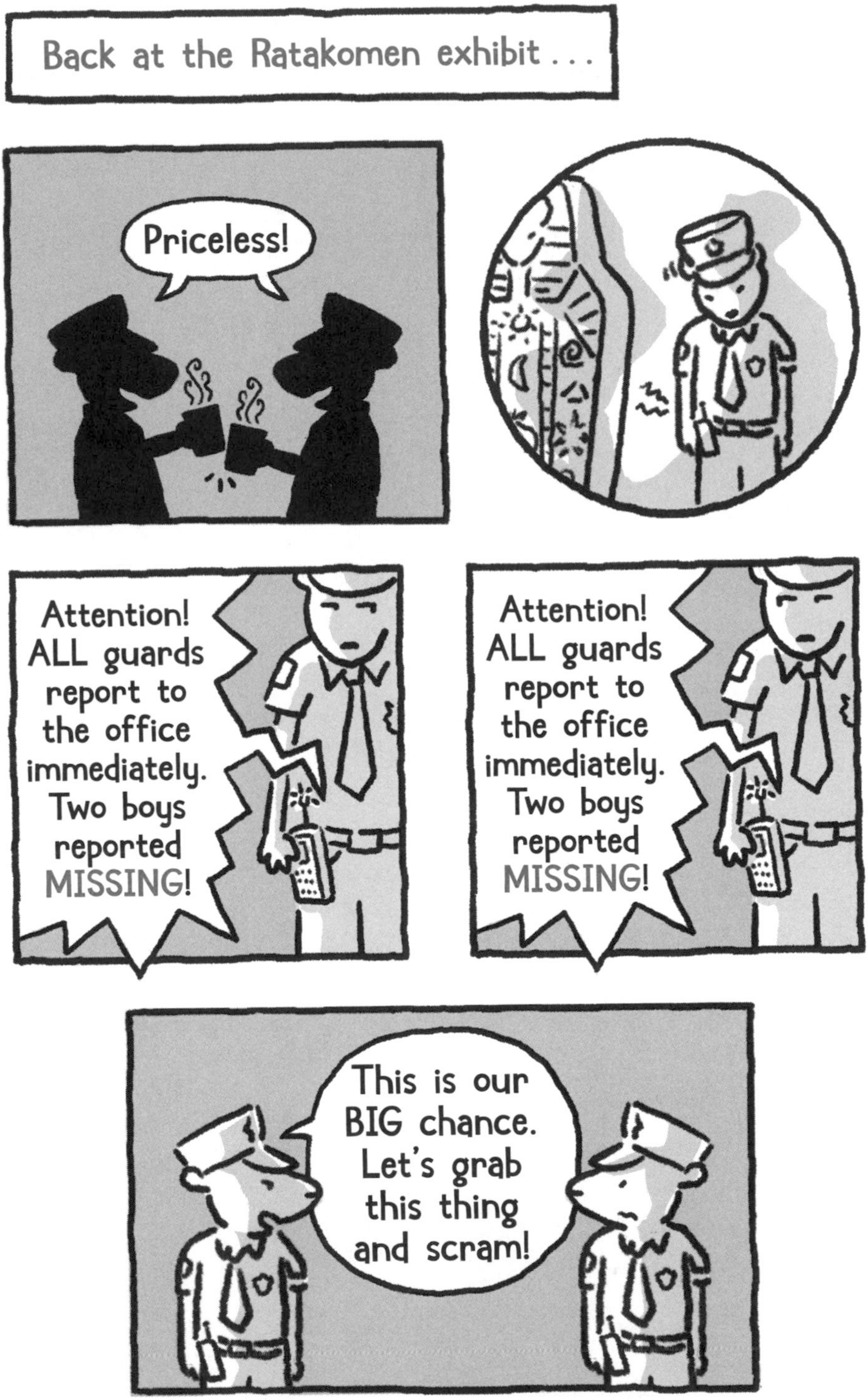
Back at the Ratakomen exhibit . . .
Priceless!
Attention! ALL guards report to the office immediately. Two boys reported MISSING!
Attention! ALL guards report to the office immediately. Two boys reported MISSING!
This is our BIG chance. Let's grab this thing and scram!

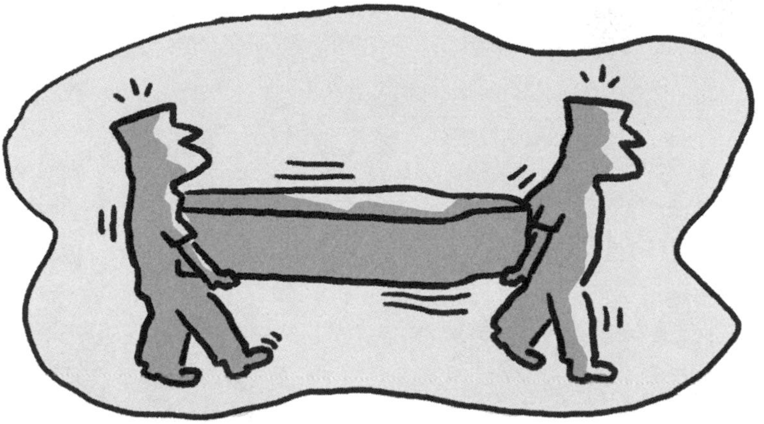

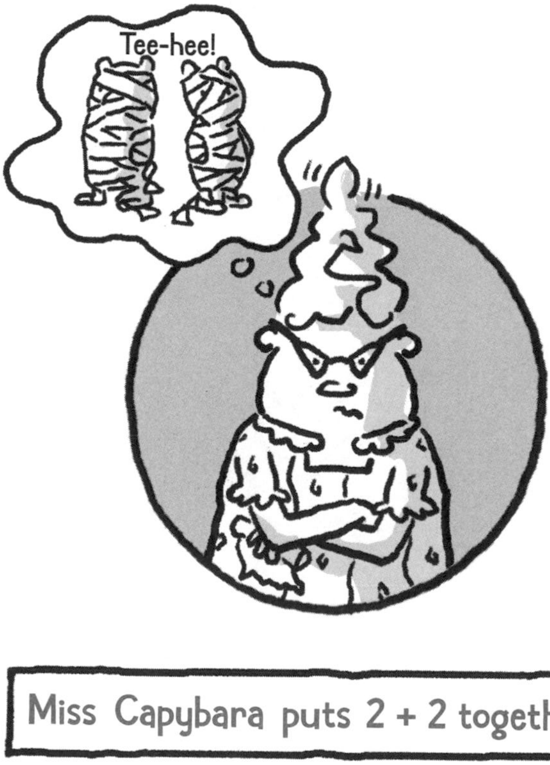
Tee-hee!

Miss Capybara puts 2 + 2 together . . .

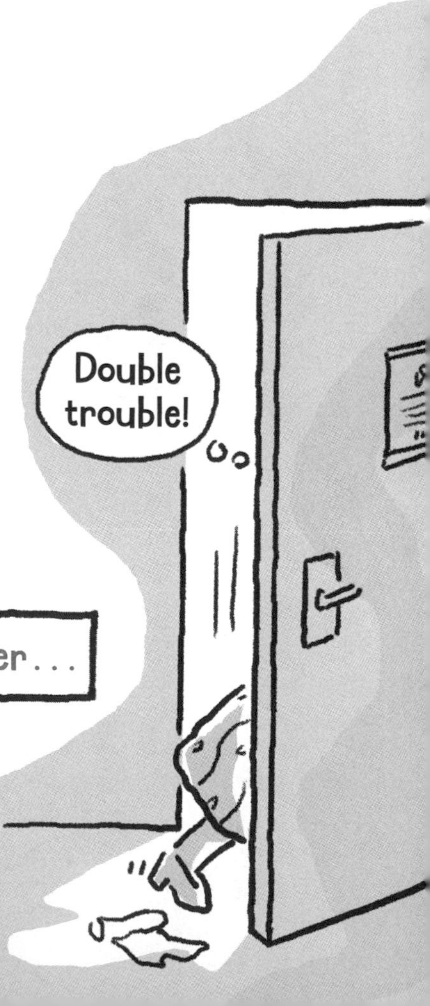
Double trouble!

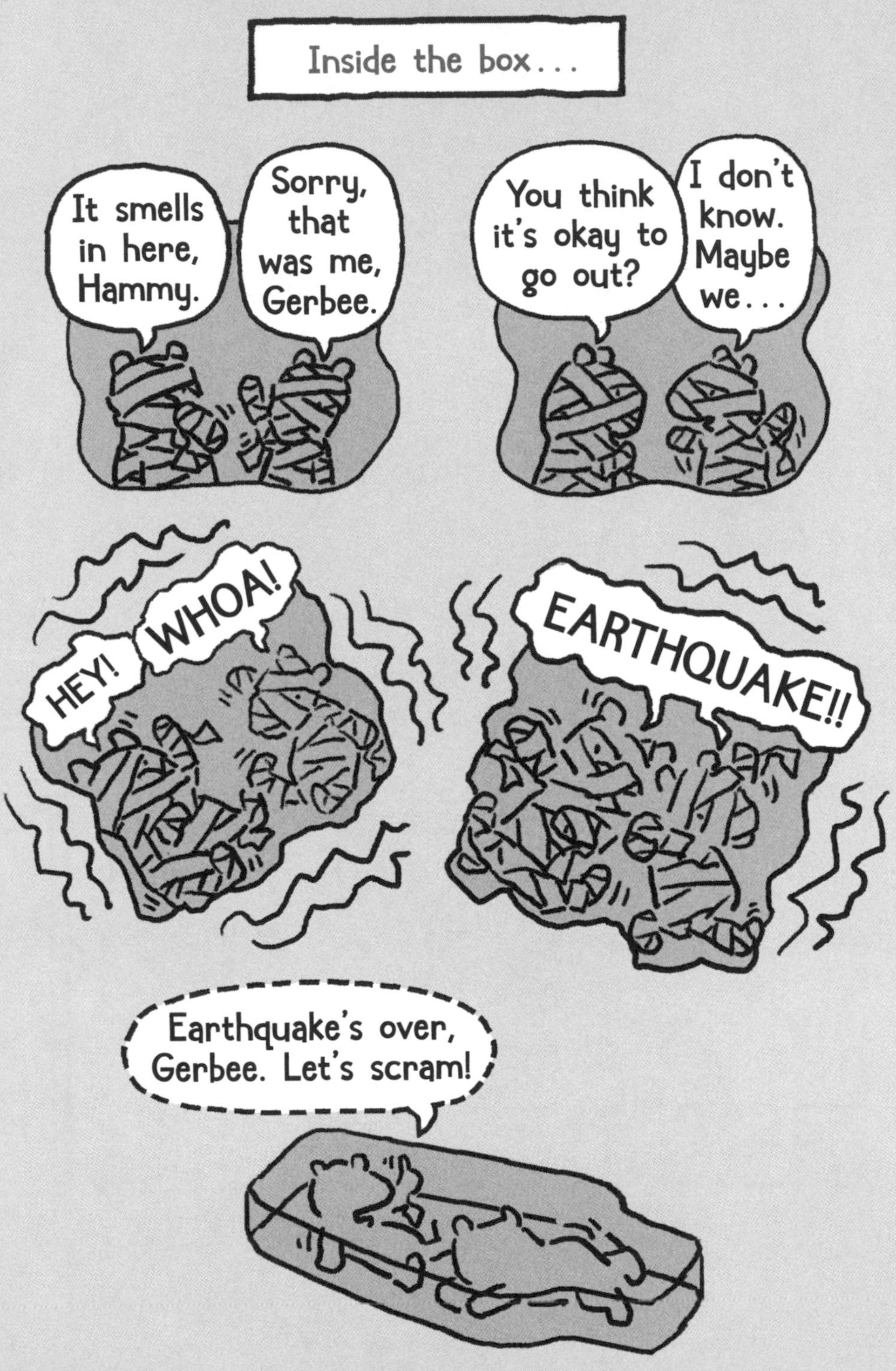
Inside the box...
It smells in here, Hammy.
Sorry, that was me, Gerbee.
You think it's okay to go out?
I don't know. Maybe we...
HEY!
WHOA!
EARTHQUAKE!!
Earthquake's over, Gerbee. Let's scram!

Outside the box...

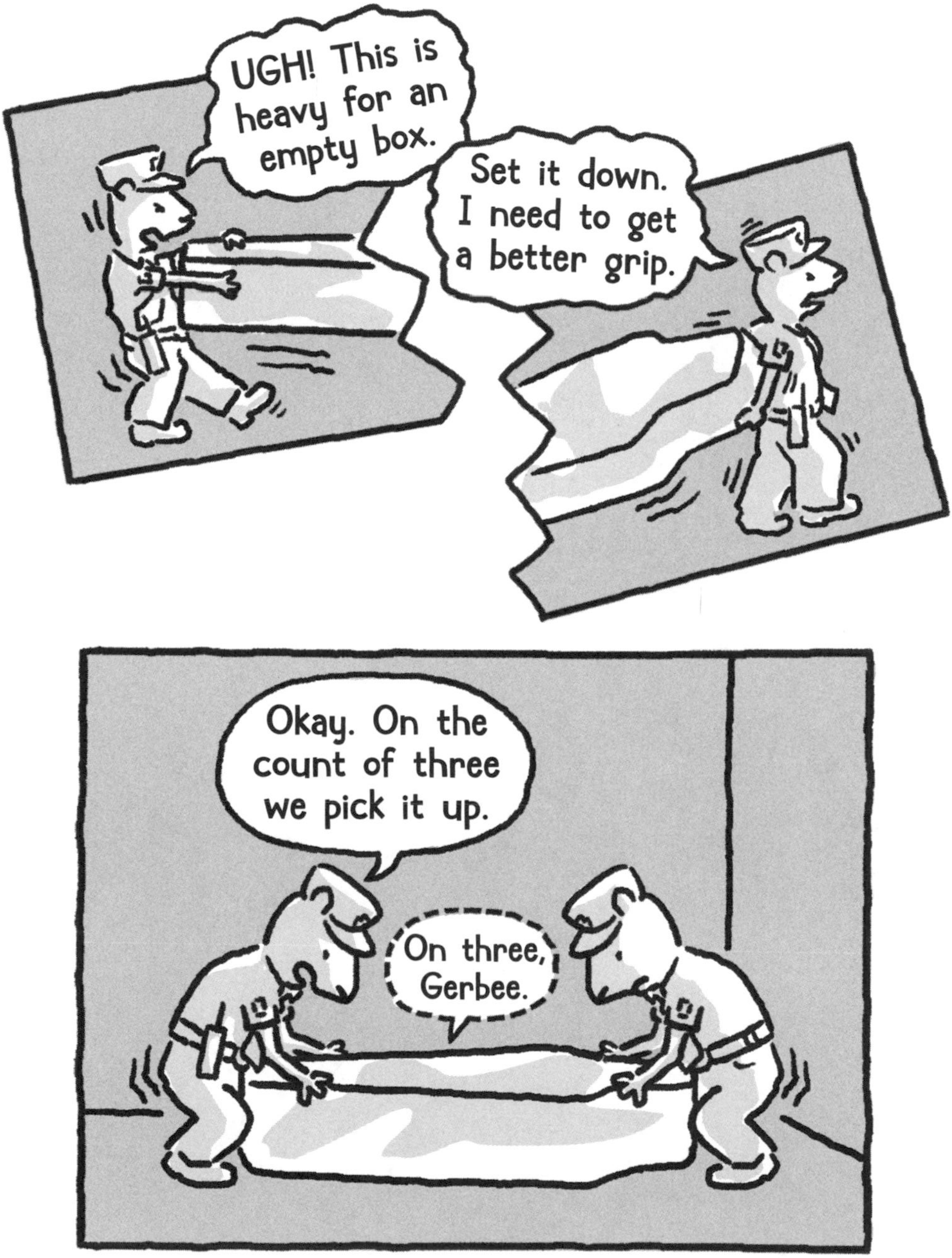
UGH! This is heavy for an empty box.
Set it down. I need to get a better grip.
Okay. On the count of three we pick it up.
On three, Gerbee.

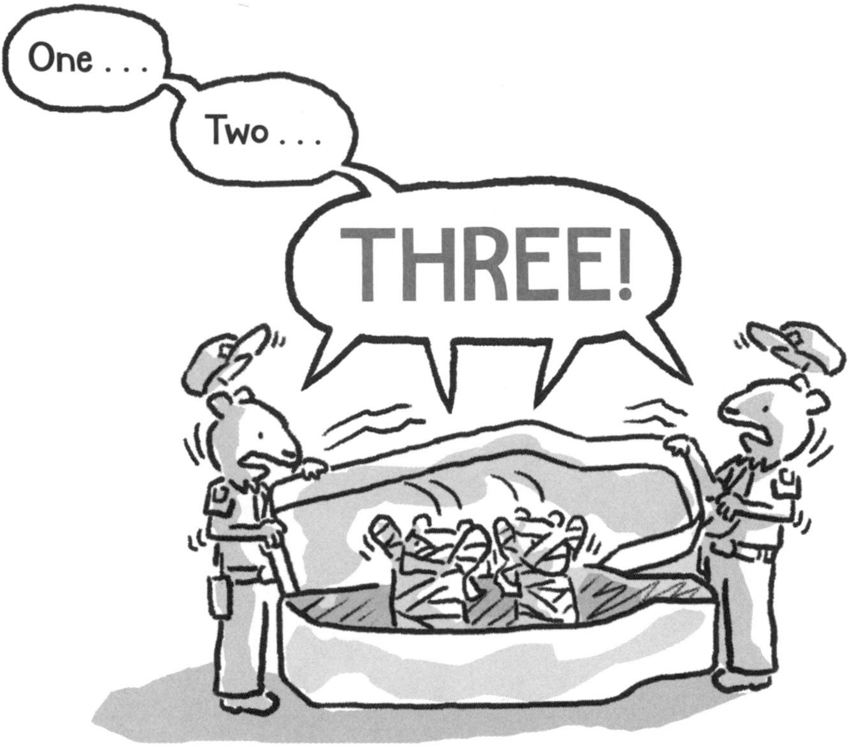
One . . .
Two . . .
THREE!

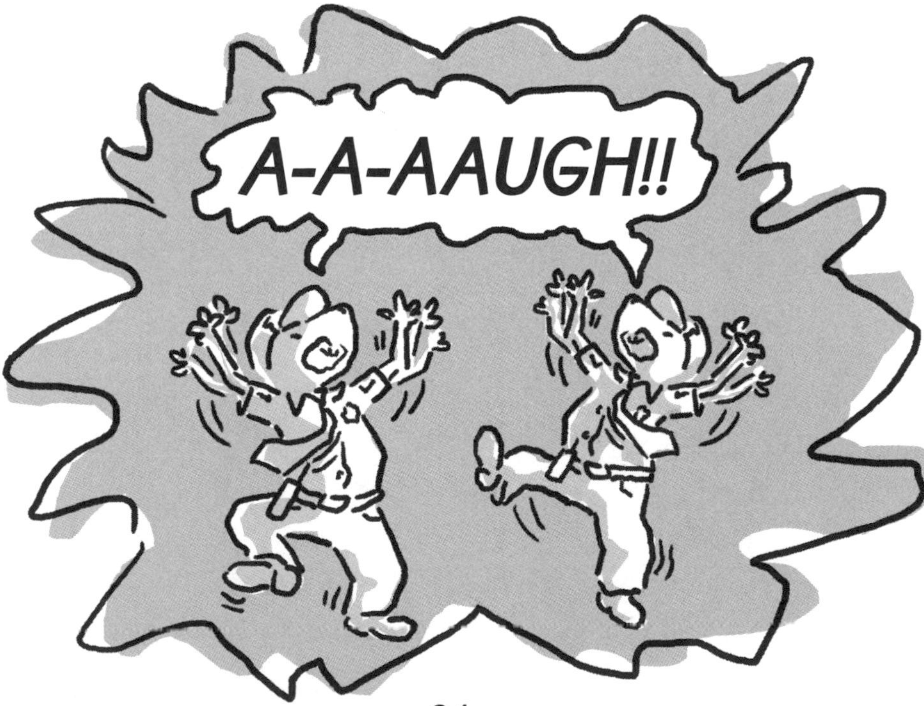
A-A-AAUGH!!

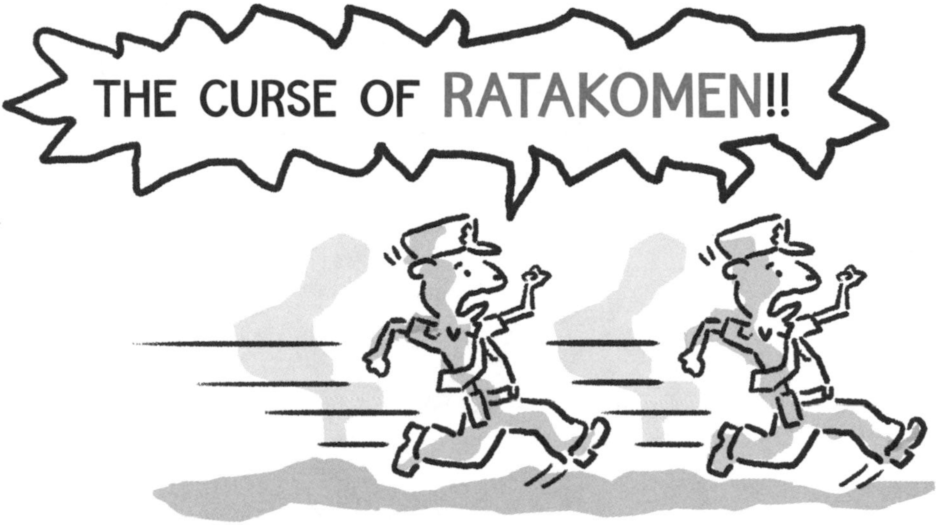
THE CURSE OF RATAKOMEN!!

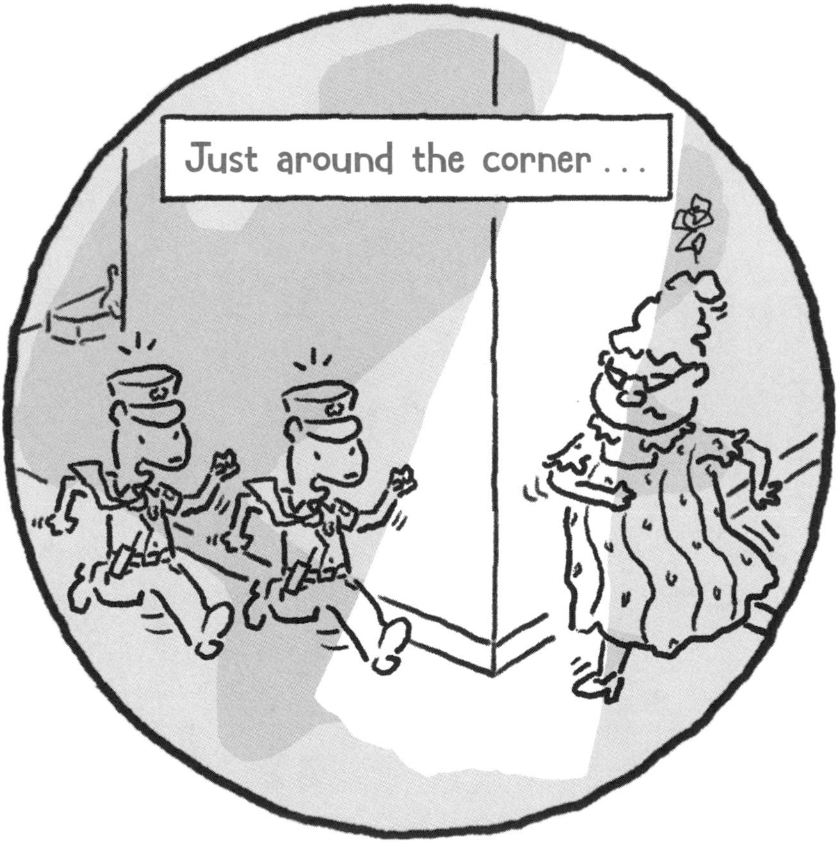
Just around the corner . . .

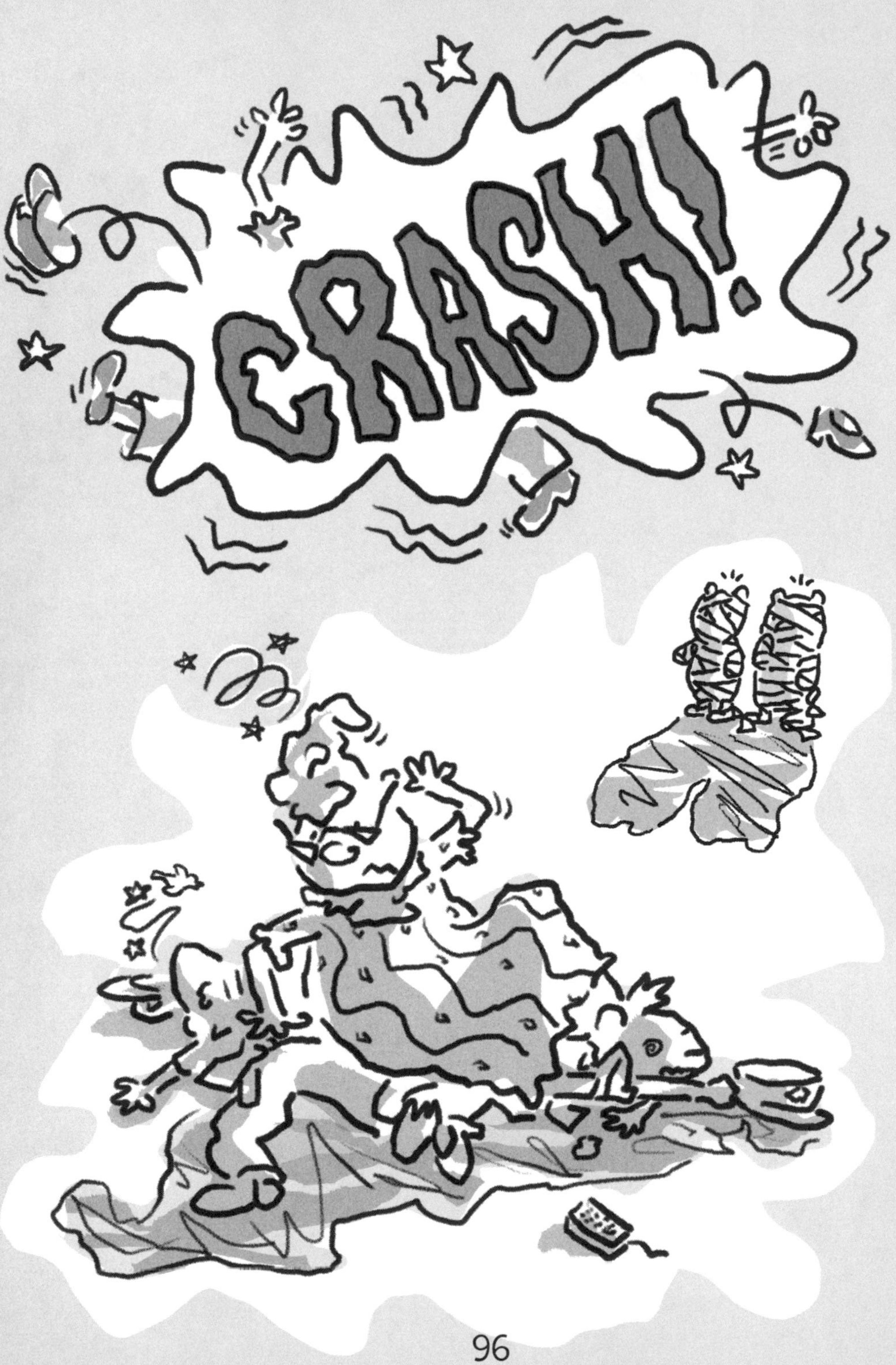
CRASH!

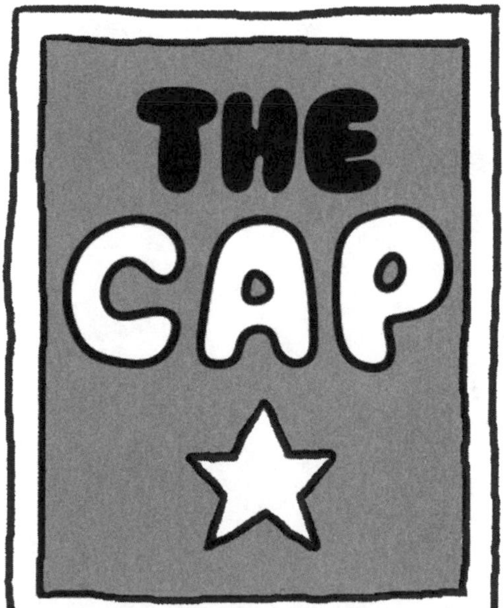
THE CAP

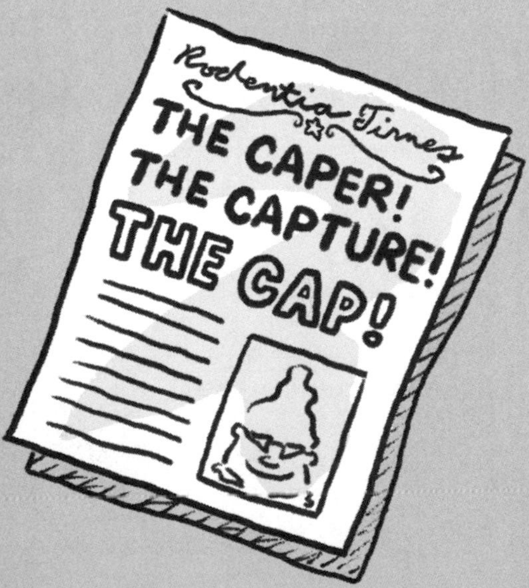
Rodentia Times
THE CAPER!
THE CAPTURE!
THE CAP!

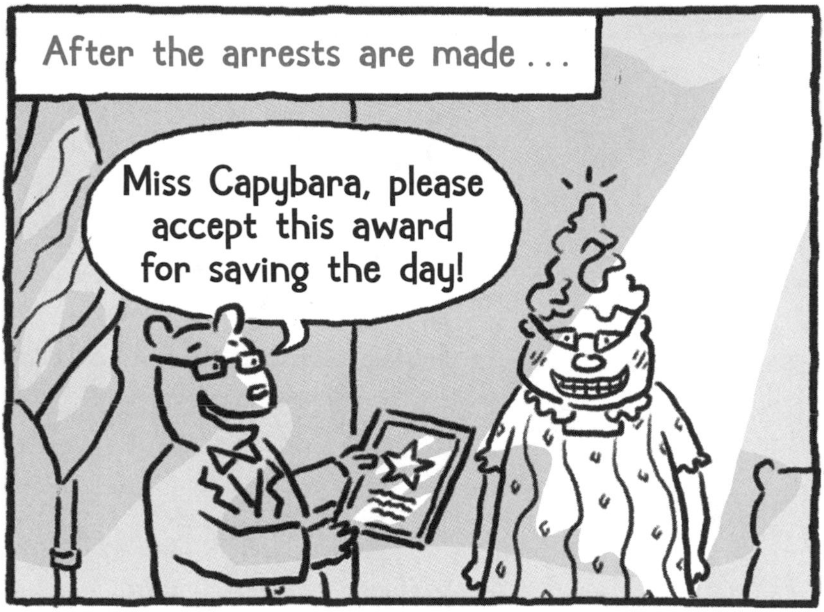
After the arrests are made . . .
Miss Capybara, please accept this award for saving the day!

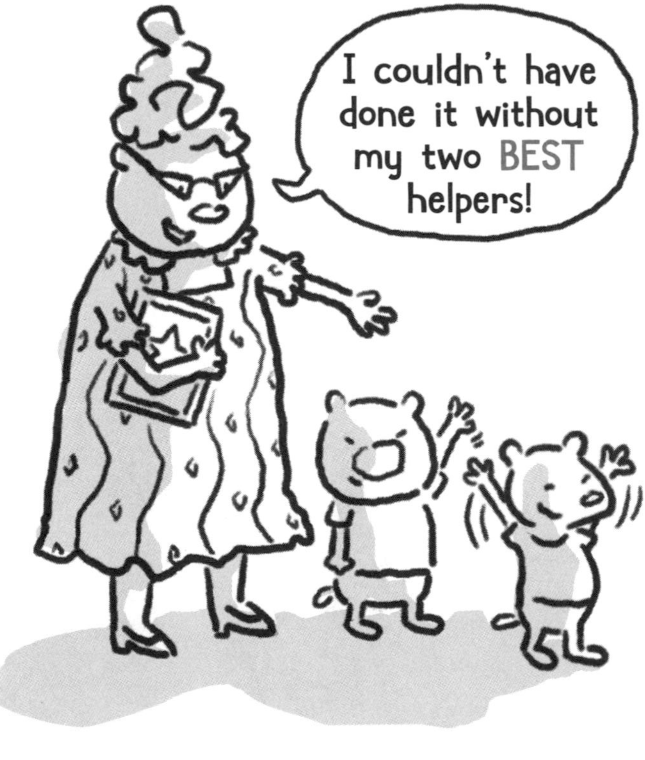
I couldn't have done it without my two BEST helpers!

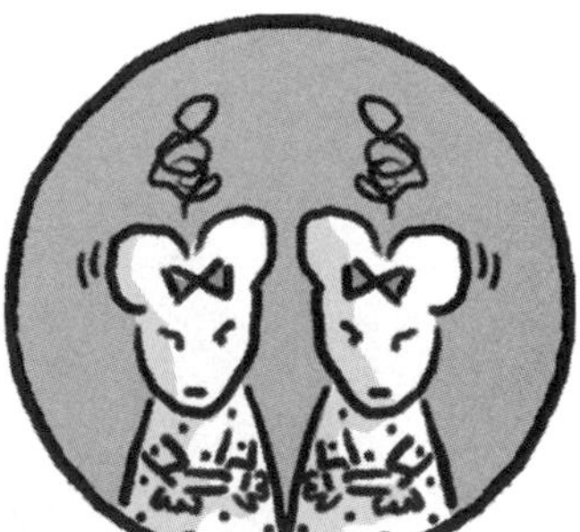

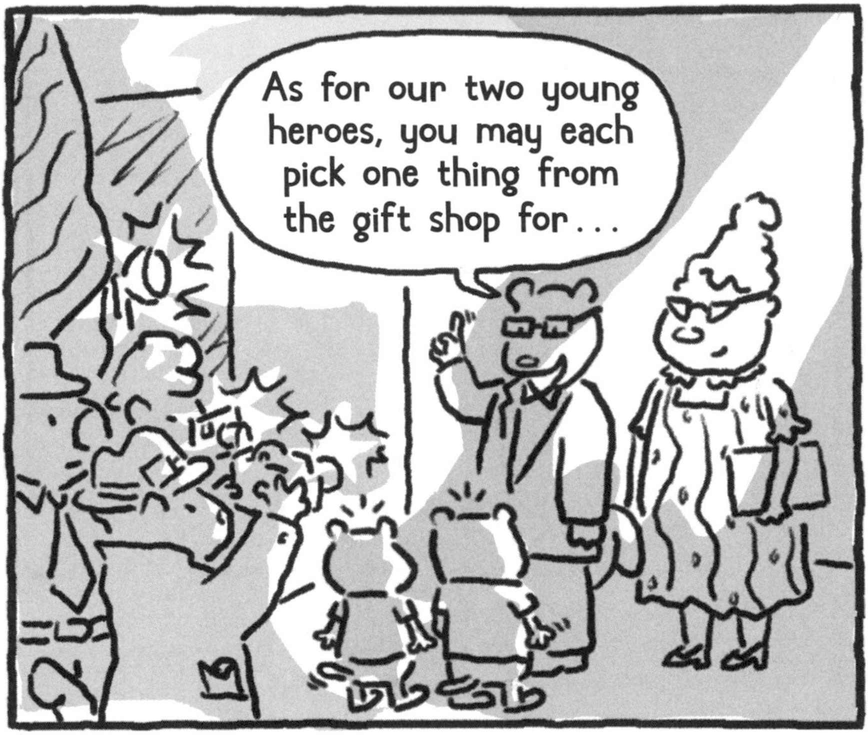
As for our two young heroes, you may each pick one thing from the gift shop for...

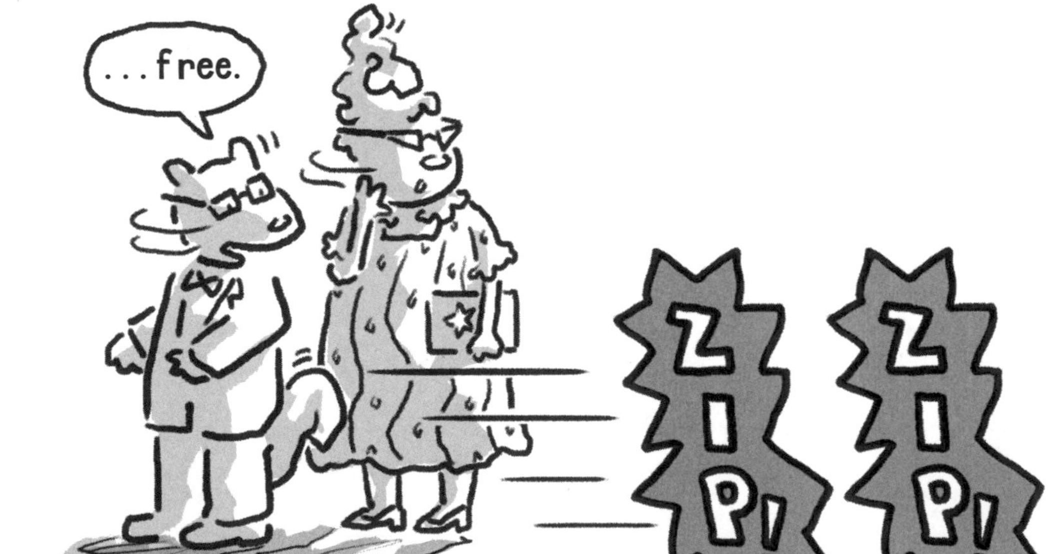
...free.
ZIP!
ZIP!

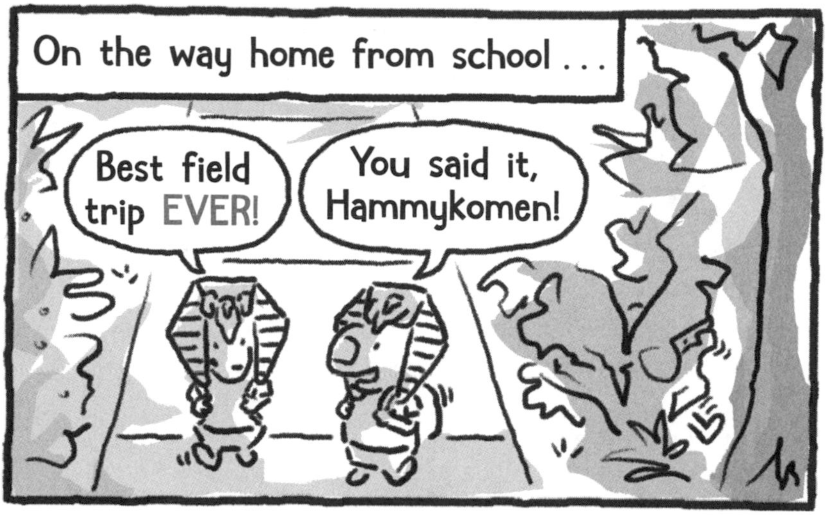
On the way home from school . . .
Best field trip EVER!
You said it, Hammykomen!

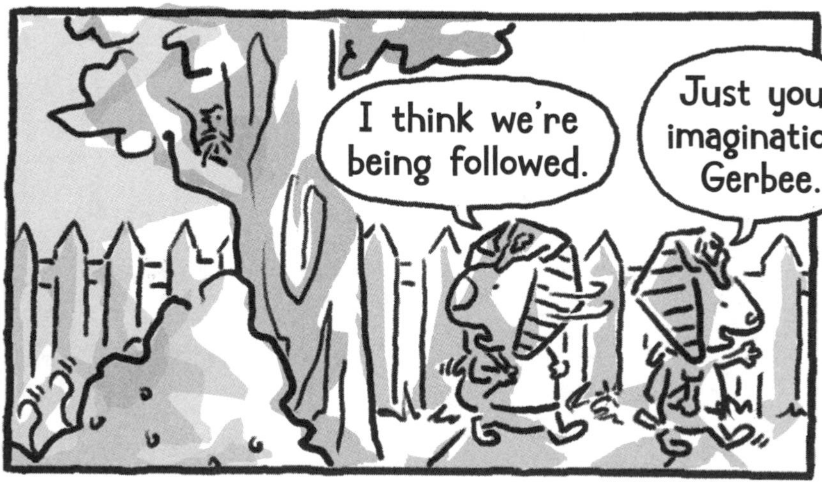
I think we're being followed.
Just your imagination, Gerbee.

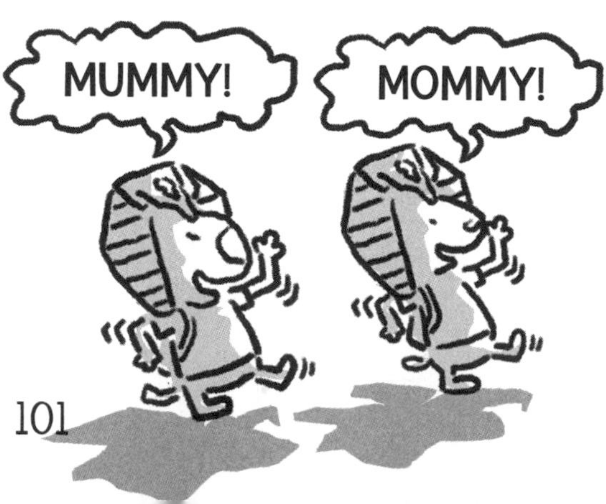
MUMMY!
MOMMY!

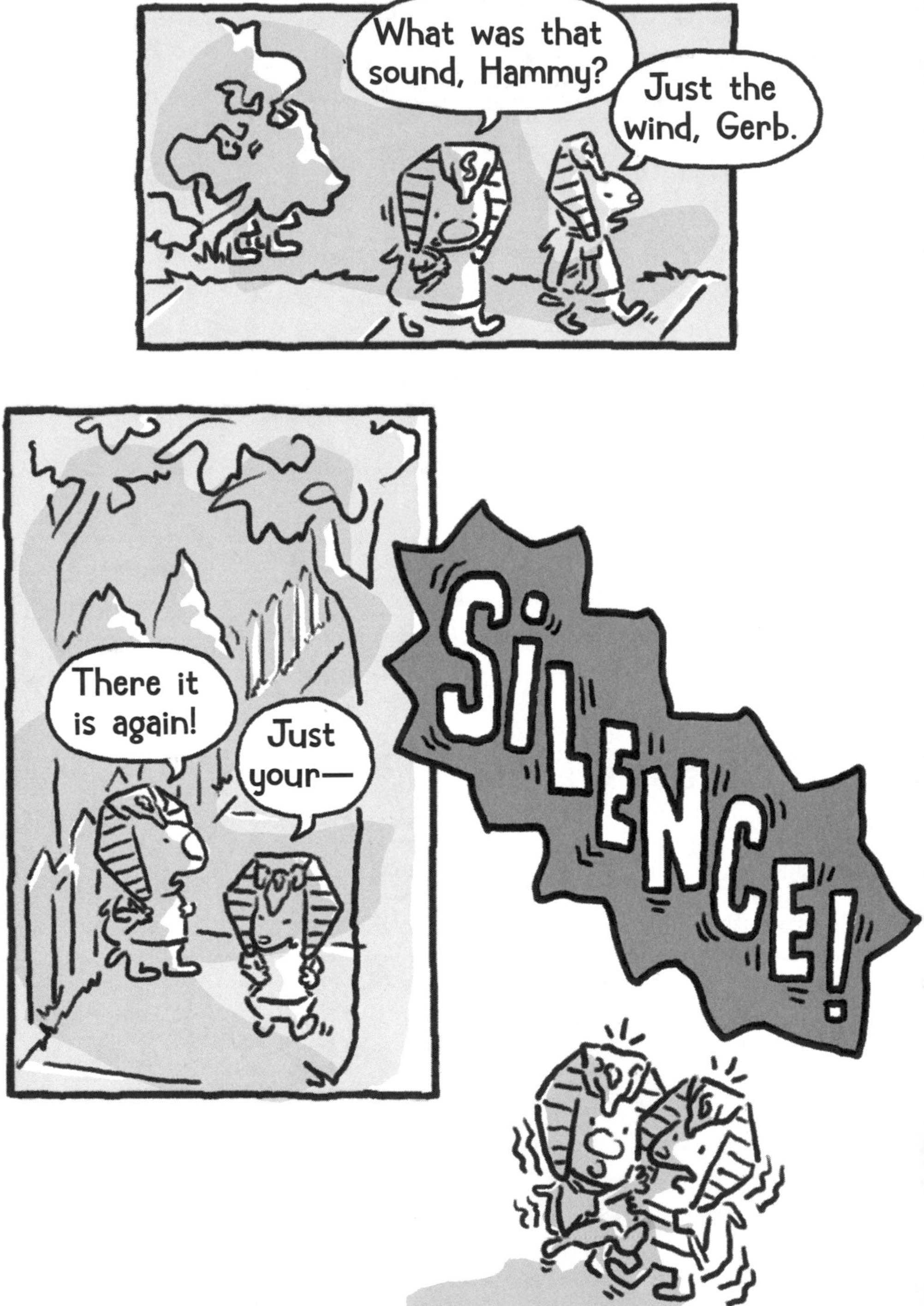
What was that sound, Hammy?
Just the wind, Gerb.
There it is again!
Just your—
SILENCE!

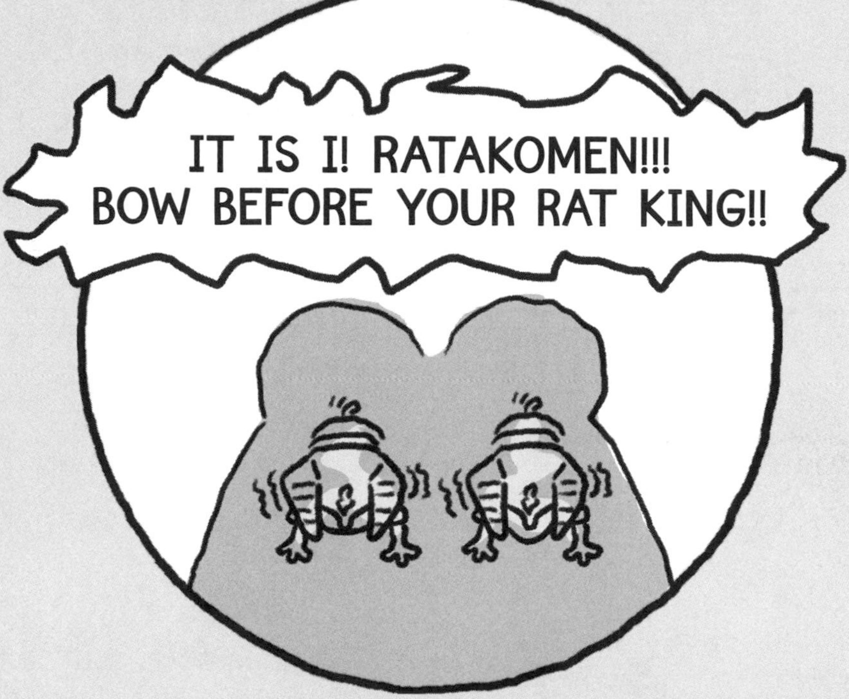
IT IS I! RATAKOMEN!!!
BOW BEFORE YOUR RAT KING!!

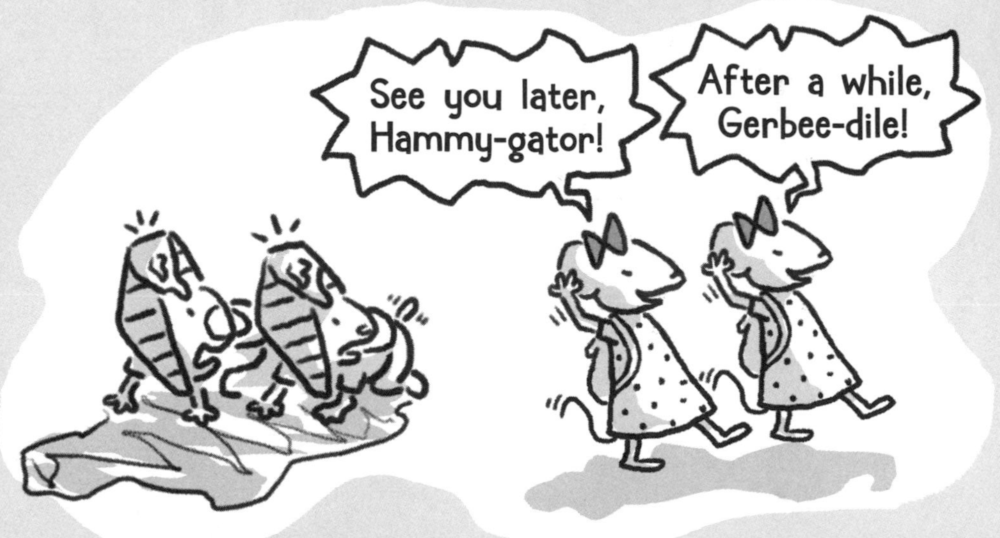
See you later, Hammy-gator!
After a while, Gerbee-dile!

THE END

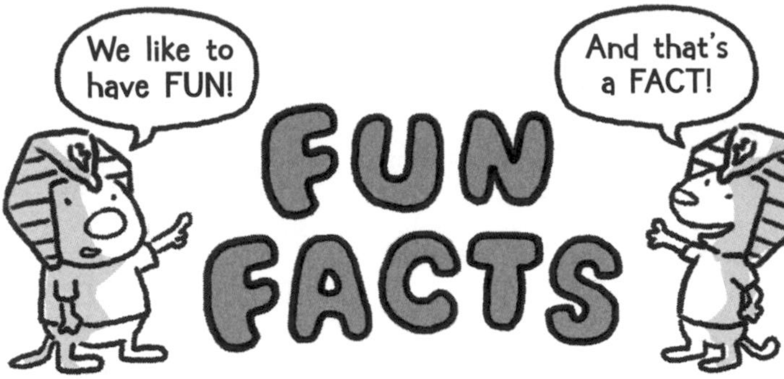
We like to have FUN!
And that's a FACT!
FUN FACTS

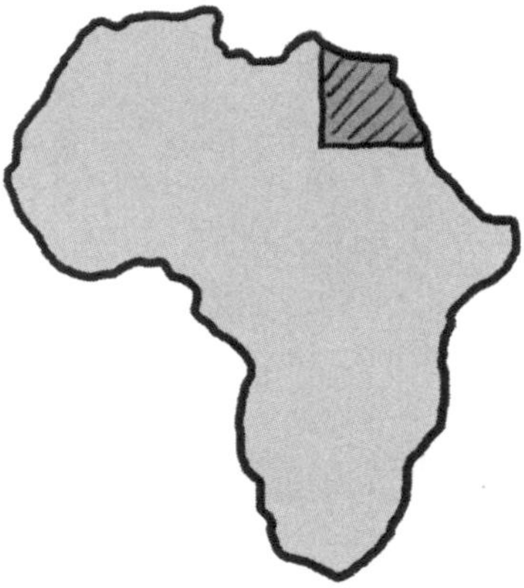

EGYPT

A country in northeastern Africa.

THE PYRAMIDS OF GIZA

There are three of them. They are made from blocks of stone. Inside are the tombs of pharaohs and queens.

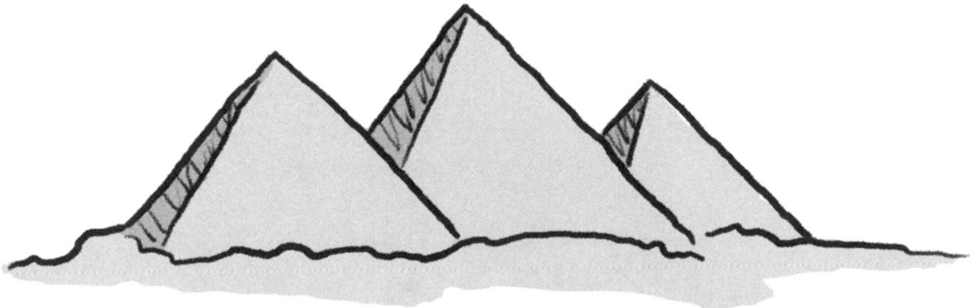

SARCOPHAGUS

The box that holds the mummy. It is made of stone and usually has decorations carved on the outside of it.

HIEROGLYPHS

Pictures or symbols that represent words.

Look, Gerbee! I'm a sphinx.

I'm a pharaoh.

SPHINX

An Egyptian stone figure with a lion's body and a human or animal head.

KING TUTANKHAMUN

King Tut was known as the boy king. He was just nine when he became king. He ruled for ten years. His coffin was made of gold. The mask he wore was too.

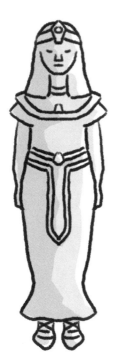

CLEOPATRA

Cleopatra was the last pharaoh of ancient Egypt. She took over the throne at eighteen when her father Ptolemy XII died. As queen she ruled for twenty-one years.

CAT MUMMIES

In ancient Egypt, cats were important. They were thought to have magical powers.

NILE RIVER

The Nile runs through Egypt. It is the longest river in the world.

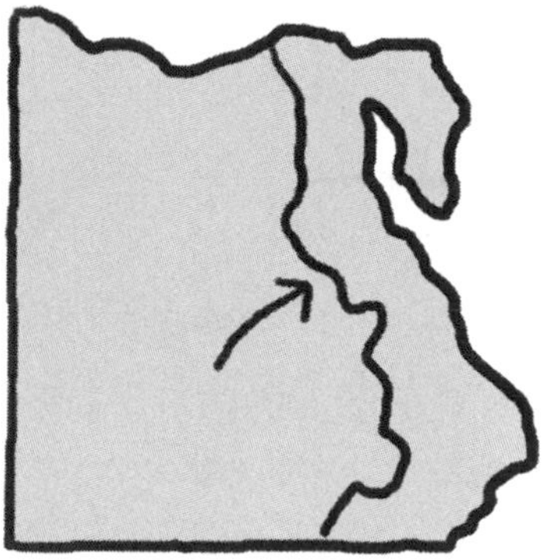

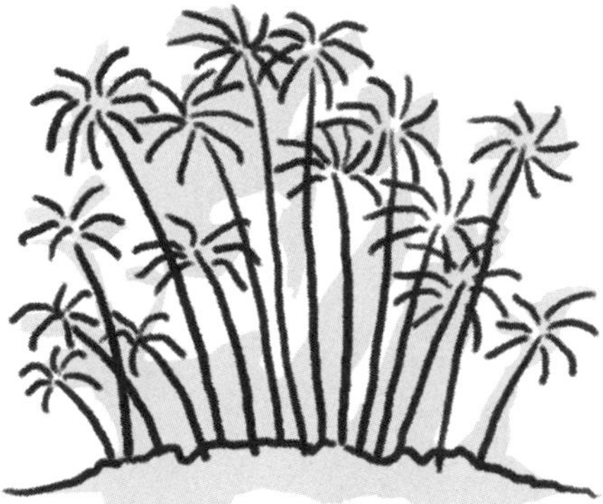

PAPYRUS

A weed found growing on the banks of the Nile. Ancient Egyptians used it to make many things, like paper and rope.

NILE CROCODILE

A reptile that can grow to twenty feet long. A real danger to ancient Egyptians.

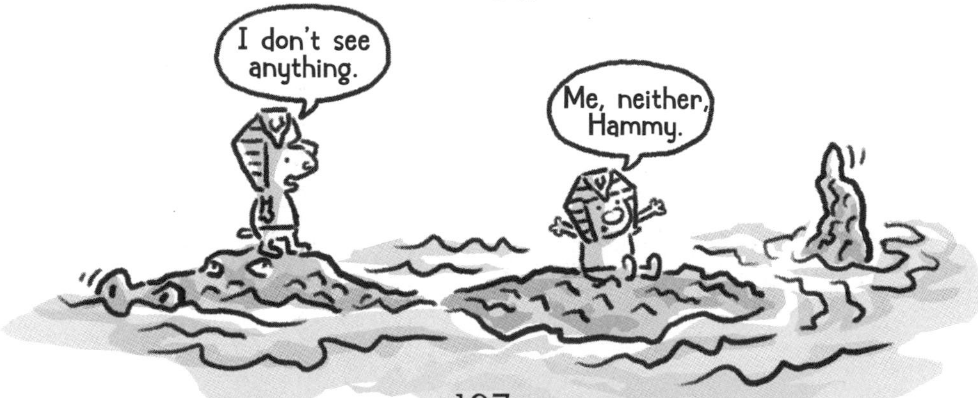
I don't see anything.
Me, neither, Hammy.

COMING SOON!

More adventures with Hammy and Gerbee!